M.I.A.

Michael Allen
Dymmoch

DIVERSIONBOOKS

Also by Michael Allen Dymmoch

The Fall

Caleb & Thinnes Mysteries
The Man Who Understood Cats
The Death of Blue Mountain Cat
Incendiary Designs
The Feline Friendship
White Tiger

Diversion Books
A Division of Diversion Publishing Corp.
443 Park Avenue South, Suite 1008
New York, New York 10016
www.DiversionBooks.com

For more information, email info@diversionbooks.com

First Diversion Books edition January 2015.
Print ISBN: 978-1-62681-940-5
eBook ISBN: 978-1-62681-507-0

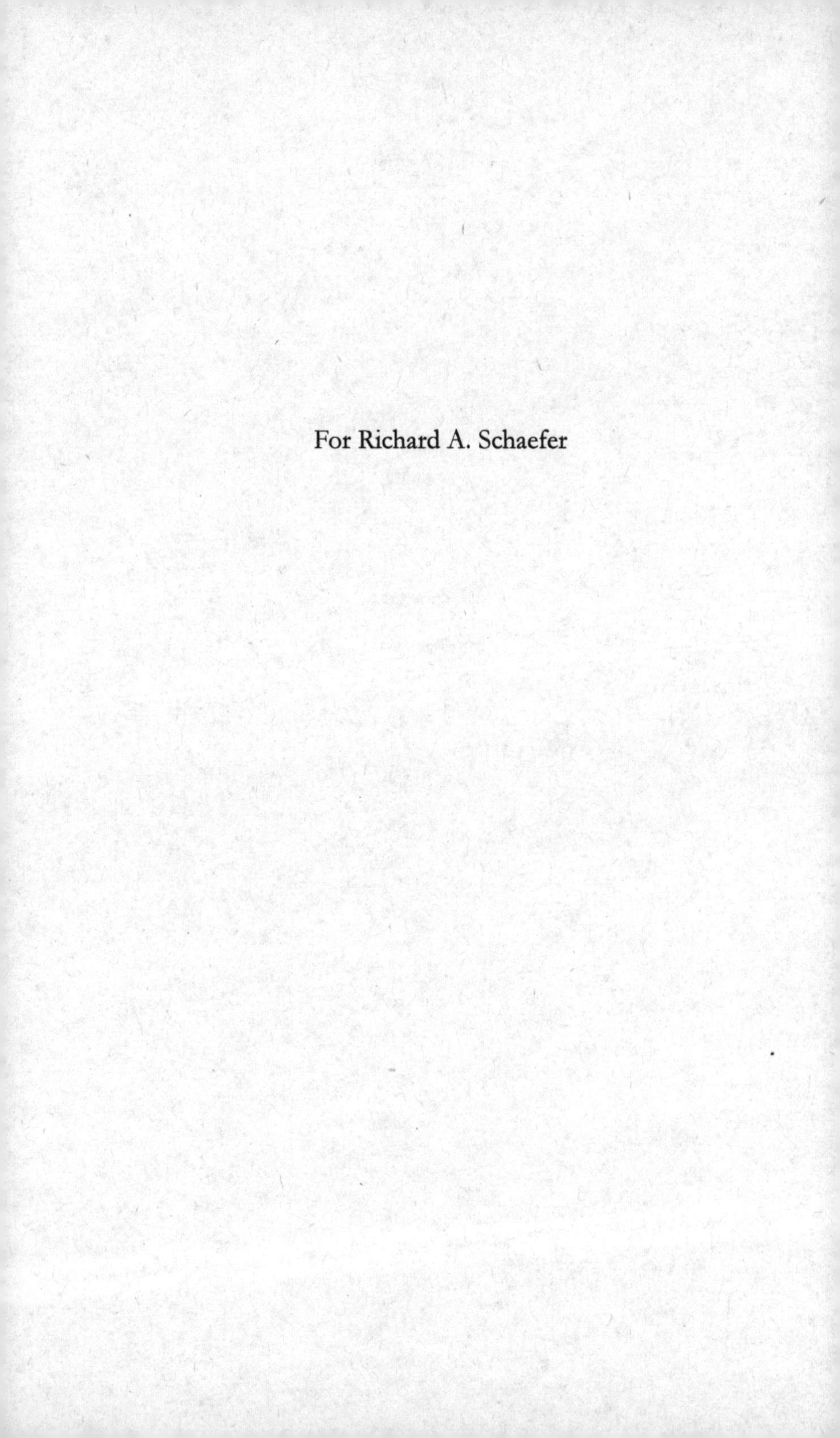

For Richard A. Schaefer

My dad died the spring I was seventeen.

Mickey Fahey was a state cop. It was a rainy Monday and he was directing traffic around an earlier accident when some moron in a Suburban lost it on the rain-slick road. They don't suspend the laws of physics just 'cause you got four-wheel drive. Two tons of vehicle doing fifty versus two hundred pounds of cop standing still. You do the math.

The cops do funerals right. A couple hundred showed up in uniform. Chicago sent a troop of bagpipers in kilts. After it was over my mom and I were left with a flag and a big hole in our lives. She lost her husband. I lost my best friend.

—from the journal of J. W. Fahey

Rhiann

"Mrs. Fahey?"

"Yes."

"This is Assistant Principal Lodge at the high school. Your son didn't come to school today."

I felt my world disintegrate. Again. I said, "I know. I'm sorry. I was supposed to call. He's ill." That last word sounded so alien. But honest. Not a lie, like "He's sick"; Jimmy wasn't sick except at heart. Heartsick. Not physically disabled. Psychically.

I said, "We've all been a little off since his dad died."

"I'm sorry," she said. It sounded mechanical. "Have you considered having him see our psychologist?"

"Not your fault," I said. I let her question go unanswered.

There was a long pause. Like when someone says something so out of line no one knows what to say.

She finally managed, "Well, thanks for calling." I didn't bother to remind her that I hadn't.

I called home as soon as I hung up. There was no answer. I left a message: "Jimmy, we have to talk. If you're not there when I get home, I'll have to report you missing."

He knew I would. Mickey had hit on that method when Jimmy was fourteen and inclined to disappear. Mickey would call all the numbers we'd collected from Jimmy's friends and ask if they'd seen Jimmy. None had, of course. But Mickey would ask them to pass along a message: If we didn't find him soon, we'd have to report his absence to the police.

Usually, Jimmy would call home before Mickey got to the bottom of the list. After a while, Jimmy stopped disappearing.

He was in the family room when I got home from work, lying on the couch upside down, with his knees hooked over the couch back. "Hi ya, Ma," he said.

There was a half-empty Jack Daniel's bottle on the floor. Yesterday, it had been nearly full.

He waited upside down. I just stood and stared. Finally, he said, "Aren't you gonna bitch me out?"

"You'll have a doozy of a hangover. That ought to be enough."

He groaned and shifted to a horizontal position, dangling his left arm on the floor.

"Why do you have to be so…? So…?"

"Reasonable?"

"Yeah."

I shook my head and went across to the kitchen to dump the whiskey down the drain. The family room is sort of an extension of the kitchen, separated from it by a large counter we sometimes use as a table. I went to the liquor cabinet, gathered up all the bottles, and emptied them as well.

Jimmy rolled on his side and put his head on his arm. "I could get more."

"Will that help?"

I could see the tears come. He buried his face.

"Jimmy, what is it you want?"

"I want Dad." He started sobbing. He jumped up and ran for the bathroom, slamming the door.

I sat on the couch and fought my own tears. I wanted Mickey, too.

"Ma, tell me about my first dad." He was over the heaves and had cleaned himself up. He was lying on the couch again with his head on my lap.

I stroked his hair. "He was a good man. Brave. Loyal."

"You always say that. I need details."

"I didn't know him well."

Jimmy put his arm over his eyes. "I thought you grew up together."

"We weren't grown-up. I was younger than you when we married. I didn't know myself, much less Billy. And he was only eighteen."

"So why did you?" He raised his arm just enough to look at me for an answer.

"He was going to war. We were more idealistic than smart. We were going to live forever. Together. But we never talked about what that meant." I shrugged. "I think we also knew he might not come back. We never talked about that, either."

Jimmy was dozing, still on the couch, and I was halfway through making dinner, chopping parsley for tabbouleh salad, when the back doorbell rang. I looked out the kitchen window at the drive that runs from the street to the garage behind our house. There was a sheriff's police cruiser parked there.

Rory Sinter was at the back door, hat in hand. "Afternoon, Rhiann," he said through the screen door. He was Mickey's buddy. Had been. I hadn't seen him since the funeral.

I nodded at him. "Rory."

He was almost as tall as Mickey, six feet at least. One of those blond men who's always unnaturally red because he's too macho to wear sunscreen. He stepped close enough to the screen to brush it with his duty belt. He tried the doorknob even before asking, "Can I come in?" The door was locked.

"What brings you up this way?" I asked.

"Mickey was my best friend." He tried the knob again. "I'd be a hell of a pal if I didn't look in on his widow now'n then."

I remembered asking Mickey what he saw in Rory. Mickey had said, "He doesn't have any other friends." He did have a wife.

He pushed the door handle again. Reluctantly, I unlatched the door, then retreated behind the counter to resume chopping. I was using the big French chef's knife I gave Mickey last Christmas.

Rory walked over to the counter and watched me for a while. As I brushed the parsley into a bowl and reached for a tomato, he said, "If there's anything you need…"

"I need Mickey." As soon as I said it, I was sorry.

"I know I'm not Mickey—"

"No, you're not."

He didn't get it. "But if you need someone to talk to..." The way he said it let me know he was offering more than conversation.

"I'm not lonely. I've got Jimmy." I looked pointedly at the couch where my son slept fitfully.

Rory must have realized for the first time that I wasn't alone. He seemed embarrassed. He edged toward the door. "Well, you got my number if you need anything."

"I do. Thanks." I stood there, holding the knife on the cutting board until he closed the door behind him.

A week later, I was weeding around my rosebushes when the real estate company's handyman came by to mow the lawn next door. The house and the rehabbed barn that served as a garage, to the west of ours, were all that remained of a farm subdivided years earlier. More recent owners had changed the siding, replaced the windows, added a dormer and veranda, and relandscaped around the house and the five-hundred-year-old oaks surrounding it. But it was still a fairly ugly structure that stood out among the surrounding homes like a cow at a dog show. Whitewashing the barn hadn't changed that, either.

The property had been for sale since March, the owners long since moved away. They'd made a deal with the realtor to maintain the place until it sold. The handyman and I had established a nodding acquaintance. When he was finished cutting the grass, he hung a CONTRACT PENDING notice under the company's FOR SALE sign.

"Who'd they sell it to?" I asked.

He shrugged. "Some guy got more money than sense. I heard he paid the asking price. Coulda got it for a whole lot less if he'd just held out a while."

The new neighbor moved in May first. He arrived in a twenty-four-foot U-Haul truck, towing a beat-up Jeep. I was sitting on the front porch, skimming the paper, when he curbed the U-Haul next door and jumped out to unhitch the Jeep. He was tall and tan and very thin. His beard and hair were nearly white—prematurely, I'd say, because he moved like a much younger man. He was dressed to work—navy T-shirt, ratty Levi's, and scuffed work boots. He left the Jeep at the curb and backed the truck into and down the drive on the first try.

The driver jumped out, and a twenty-something kid joined him from the other side. They opened the barn doors, and the man backed the truck far enough inside so that I couldn't see what they unloaded—lots of stuff, apparently. It was half an hour before the man pulled the truck up to the veranda steps of the house, and the kid closed the barn.

It took longer for them to get the furniture inside. Everything looked like the good stuff, mostly wood and heavy. Expensive. There wasn't a whole lot—dressers, disassembled beds, tables, chairs, a broad modern desk—but they had to maneuver it up the porch steps. Presumably, some of it had to go up the narrow stairs and around corners to be distributed among the upper rooms.

Then there were boxes, grocery-store giveaways by the labels—the kind you packed the contents of your drawers and shelves in, and your kitchen equipment. Some of the boxes seemed heavy—books perhaps. There was the large black-spotted white carton of a Gateway computer. The printer and stereo equipment were easy to identify—no packaging at all.

All in all it, seemed like hot work for just two men. I went inside and put together a tray—plastic tumblers, ice bucket, assorted pops, and a pitcher of iced tea.

I got to the foot of the veranda steps just as the movers were coming out for more boxes, the elder in the lead. He stopped when he noticed me. He seemed startled.

Up close, he didn't look any older than me, despite deep furrows over his brows, extensive crow's-feet, and the snow-white hair. It was off his collar and ears, but long enough to hang over his forehead, like Elvis. His beard—what would've been termed a goatee if it were longer—was neatly trimmed. The skin on his arms was pocked with tiny white scars, dozens of them; crown-of-thorns tattoos circled his biceps, showing below his sleeves like heavy dark lace.

"Hi," I said, "I'm Rhiann Fahey. Next door. Could you use something cold?"

"Sure could," the man said. He stepped quickly down the steps to take the tray from me. He handed it to the boy, and lifted a box down from the back of the truck. He put the box on the veranda; the boy balanced the tray on top.

The man offered me his hand. "I'm John Devlin, your new neighbor."

I shook his hand; he had a warm, firm grip. He said, "This is Davey, Mrs. Fahey, my assistant."

I wondered how he knew I was Mrs., but I quickly remembered my wedding ring.

Davey nodded and said, "Pleased to meet you." He was my height and stocky, with crew-cut blond hair and green eyes. He was dressed in the same uniform as his boss, sans tattoos. He looked longingly at the pop cans.

"Please, help yourself," I told him.

He took a Coke, popped it open, and drank most of it down in one long gulp. Then he swallowed a belch and nodded appreciatively.

John helped himself to a tumbler and handed one to me. He pointed to the tray and waved his finger back and forth at it, raising his eyebrows.

"Iced tea," I told him.

He filled my tumbler, then his own. We helped ourselves to ice cubes. I held up my drink. "Welcome to the neighborhood."

John said, "Thanks." He took a drink and added, "This hits the spot."

I had the strongest feeling of déjà vu. "Have we met before?"

He gave me a dazzling smile that vanished before he said, "Maybe in a former life."

John

I have always hated spring. In the spring of 1987, I decided I would change my attitude. New house, new neighborhood, new neighbors. Maybe I could muster a new feeling about the season.

The house on Cemetery Road was "a charming traditional farmhouse" according to the real estate agent, an eyesore, as far as I could see. But it was situated on an acre lot and had the most essential features: Location. Location. Location.

The place came with neighbors: Rhiann Fahey and her son. She was widowed, the real estate agent said. She had a melancholy expression when she thought no one was looking. Up close, she was exquisite—Black Irish with pale skin and raven hair, intensely blue eyes. Made me want to grab my camera or a sketchpad.

When she came over with iced tea and sodas, she solved the problem of how to introduce myself. I wondered how long she'd grieve for her dead husband. And if she'd notice me when she was done.

Jimmy

"Did you ever wonder if you were adopted?" I asked Finn one day. Finn and I have been best friends since the seventh grade. We were hanging out in the McDonald's parking lot, leaning on the hood of my '77 Chevy.

"No," Finn said. He ran his fingers through his carrot-colored hair. "I look just like my dad. All I gotta do is look in the mirror." He stared at me. "Why'd ya ask? You *know* you were adopted."

"Yeah," I said. "Since Dad died, I've been wondering about my birth father. When I ask Ma about him, she gets real vague."

"Maybe they didn't get along."

"She said they did."

Finn shrugged. "Anyway, why do you have to get it from her?"

"'Cause *he's* been MIA eighteen years. I'm not gonna find out anything from him."

"He wasn't MIA before he went missing, was he? I mean, he was born on this planet, wasn't he?"

"Finding that out could be more work than a term paper."

Finn's always been better in school than me. Research is a game for him. He grinned. "How bad do you want to know?" He pulled out his Camels. "I bet if you were trying to find out what your mom got you for Christmas, you wouldn't have a problem." He shook one halfway out of the pack, holding it out.

I waved it away. "No, thanks, man."

He shrugged. He grabbed the cigarette with his lips and pulled it free, then put the pack away and lit up.

I waited while he took a long drag and blew the smoke out in rings. "Those things'll stunt your growth, man."

Finn laughed. He's already six inches taller than me. "Like I gotta worry. You ever ask your dad about your birth father?"

"Nah. I was afraid he'd think—I didn't want to hurt his feelings."

"I hear ya. But I bet he would've told you if you asked."

I just shrugged. Too late now.

"Too bad your ma's such a dickhead about it."

I put my fists up. "You calling my ma a dickhead?"

He shoved his cig in his mouth and held up his open hands. "No, man. You got the coolest ma in the state, or maybe the whole country. Just..." He dropped his hands and took a long drag on his cigarette. "It'd be easier if she'd just tell you."

"She's probably got her reasons."

Finn blew a huge smoke ring. "That doesn't mean you can't do a little detecting."

"Where do I even start?"

"Doesn't your ma have some old albums or love letters?"

"Love letters?"

"Yeah. My ma used to." He took another drag and dropped the cigarette, then crushed it underfoot.

"Used to?"

Finn shrugged. "She burned them after she caught me reading them. Pretty hot stuff."

"Gross!"

He laughed. "There's always your birth certificate."

"What'll that tell me—besides that I was born?"

"*Where* you were born."

"I know *that*."

"Where your folks were born. Which could lead to your birth father's parents. Get creative. I'm not gonna do everything for you. Besides, I gotta be home for dinner in fifteen minutes. And you're gonna give me a ride—if you can get that heap started."

Rhiann

I arrived at work the next morning to find a semi tractor with a forty-eight-foot trailer blocking the drive and the front door of the office. It was still there after I parked my car. The driver had left it running, so I got in and drove it to the far end of the back lot—two blocks away. By the time I hitched a ride back with Squirrel, the yard man, the trucker had come back and was on the verge of a meltdown. Frank was grinning like the Cheshire cat.

"Hey!" I yelled at the trucker. When he finally looked at me, I tossed the keys to him and said, "Relax."

It took him about ten seconds to realize what he was holding. "Where's my truck?"

I pointed to the NO PARKING, TOW ZONE sign that had been hidden by his rig.

"Where *is* it?"

"Far end of the yard."

"You shut it off!"

"Yeah."

"Bitch!"

I just raised my eyebrows.

He turned and stalked off, shaking his head, muttering, "It'll never start."

I looked at Frank, who was laughing.

He hadn't laughed the first time I reparked someone's truck. One of his senior drivers once had the bad habit of leaving his truck wherever he liked. I'd just been working for the company a month, but I was fed up with the delays he caused everyone. The day I caught him leaving it in the drive and asked him to move it, he just waved at me—annoyed—and kept on going. It made me mad, so mad I climbed in the cab and managed to get the truck in gear. I pulled it out the front gate and across the highway, and left it nosed into a farm field access drive. We'd had a very wet spring, so the driver wasn't able to turn around in the field. He was forced to wait a long time for a break in traffic before he could back out. When he stormed in demanding that Frank fire me, Frank told him it would be a lot easier to replace *him*.

"An' don't let the door hit you in the ass on your way out."

Now, I grinned at Frank and said, "Good morning."

"Mornin', Rhiann."

Frank was preoccupied with something all morning. After lunch he got out a yellow legal pad and started composing a letter. Frank hated writing anything. Unless it was a personal letter, he'd tell me the gist and have me write it. Since he didn't ask me to write this letter, I decided to leave him alone.

He went through five or six drafts, tearing each up and pitching it into the wastebasket in frustration. In between tries, he'd stare into space; once I caught him staring at me.

Just before quitting time, he came over to my desk and stood over me. "Rhiann…ah…er…"

"Spit it out, Frank."

He took a deep breath and blurted, "Are you all right?"

I must have looked as surprised as I felt because he added, "I mean, you got enough to get by on and all?"

I was touched. "Yes, Frank. Mickey had insurance."

He seemed relieved. "You ever need anything, just ask."

I said, "Thank you."

He nodded again and stalked toward the door. "I'm goin' home."

"Good night, Frank."

I wouldn't have pried into his personal business, if he hadn't missed the wastebasket with one of his failed drafts. I picked it up and couldn't resist flattening out the pieces and fitting the puzzle together.

The letter read:

> *Dear Rhiann,*
>
> *I know I could never replace Mickey in your life, but I also know being left behind is lonely. If you ever get to the point when you're ready to let another man in your life, I'd like to be the first in line to apply. I'm old but I love you. You know I could take care of you and leave you well off.*

I realized I was crying when my tears splashed on the paper. I swept the pieces up, crumpled them together, and threw them away. Then I put my head down on the desk and cried until I had no more tears.

Later, I emptied the office wastepaper baskets into the dumpster so no one else would stumble onto Frank's letters.

John

I first met Jimmy Fahey the day his ten-year-old Chevy Celebrity died in front of my drive. I watched from the porch as he tried to restart it, then struck the steering wheel in frustration. He got out and put the hood up, but didn't seem to recognize the problem. At that point, I decided to intervene.

"Need a hand?"

He stiffened and came out from under the hood with a startled expression. He was tall enough to look me in the eye, and did.

"I'm John Devlin," I said. "Your new neighbor."

"Jimmy Fahey." He stuck out his hand; I shook it. You can tell a lot about a man's character by watching how his kids behave. I never met Mickey Fahey, but the fact that his son looked me in the eye and shook my hand told me a lot about the man. "Sorry about blocking your driveway," Jimmy said.

I shrugged. "What seems to be the problem?"

He shook his head. "It just died."

"Mind if I have a look?"

"No. Go ahead."

The Chevy was clean on the outside, but under the hood it looked as if it had never been serviced. "You got gas in it?"

"Yeah. I put five bucks in yesterday."

The car had sounded to me as if it had a fuel problem. It wasn't out of gas, so maybe the filter was clogged or a fuel line blocked or the carburetor gummed up.

"Let me get a couple tools—"

"I don't want to cause you any trouble."

I didn't point out that having his car stalled in front of my drive was more of a nuisance than helping get it started. "No trouble."

The fuel filter seemed to be original equipment, and it was amazing anything had gotten through it in years. "When was the last time this thing had a tune-up?"

"I dunno. My dad got it for me for my birthday. He showed me how to change the oil and filter, but he...We never—He died."

"I'm sorry."

He just shrugged.

I could see he was fighting back tears. I changed the subject. "You could probably get it started without a fuel filter, but it won't run for long." I pulled the Jeep key out of my pocket and held it out to him. "Why don't you run down to the auto parts store and get one. And get an air filter while you're at it."

"I couldn't—"

"Sure you can. Just drive over the grass. You won't hurt it."

"I mean, I don't have any cash."

"I have an account there. Tell Jake to charge it to Black's. We can settle up later."

He thought about it for a good ten seconds. "Thanks, Mr. Devlin."

"Call me John."

The fuel filter did the trick, although the Chevy kept missing on at least two cylinders. I gave Jimmy my card: "BLACK'S AUTOMOTIVE, John Devlin, Prop."

"Why don't you come over some day after school and we can tune it up. With new plugs and points and a set of wires it should run like new."

"I don't know, Mr. Devlin. John. How would I pay you?"

"Well, you said you can change oil. You could work it off."

I thought he was going to refuse again, but he was a

normal kid. And kids that age can't resist the chance to tinker with cars.

"Thanks, John. That would be cool."

Rhiann

Late May—spring green and cloudless sky, not too hot. Perfect gardening weather. I was slathered in suntan lotion, incognito behind dark sunglasses. Saturday morning, I was weeding in the front beds and along the walk.

I'd been sitting on my feet and they were killing me. I paused to stretch. I looked up. Overhead a hawk soared, and I followed its solo flight until I lost it against the sun. Was it lonely? Had its mate fallen to an idiot hunter or an electric wire? How did it go on alone? *Oh, God, I miss Mickey!*

Tears seeped from beneath my lids.

It was always like this. I'd be okay for a week or two. Then something'd bring Mickey to mind and I'd dissolve. Would I ever get through a month without tears?

A shadow fell across the walk. I looked up into the sympathetic eyes of John Devlin. "Sorry to disturb you."

He could hardly time his visits to the lulls between my scattered bouts of grief.

"You're not disturbing me." I took off my glasses and wiped my eyes on my sleeve. "My husband died in March. I haven't quite recovered."

"I'd think that would be something from which you'd never quite recover."

I nodded. "He was a state police officer."

"The one killed in the traffic accident?"

Nodding, I bit my lip and swallowed back my tears.

"I'm sorry."

How many times had I heard that in the last few months? But he seemed sincere enough.

"Actually, I'm getting better. I used to cry all the time."

He held up a book, *Chilton's Manual for Chevrolet Celebrity*. "Your son wanted to borrow this."

He looked around at the flower beds. "How did you come by your green thumb?"

"Mickey—my husband—gave me a Peace rose for Mother's Day, when Jimmy was three. He said he was too cheap to buy flowers that would only last a week or two when for half as much he could give me flowers for a lifetime." I smiled, remembering. "Of course I didn't know the first thing about growing roses, so he bought me a book. By the time I finished reading it, I was hooked."

"Did you landscape this yourself?"

"Oh, yeah."

"It's terrific."

"Well, after fifteen years or so you learn to put the tall plants in the back and to save work by planting perennials."

"You make it sound easy."

"It is, sort of. You plant everything that looks good to you, and whatever survives the season is what you get."

"I'll have to try that."

"I have a book you can borrow..."

Jimmy

Ma's always let me have a day off when I need it. Outside school, perfect attendance doesn't count for much—maybe a gold watch when you retire and don't need a watch anymore. Even though I'd already ditched five days since the funeral, she didn't give me a hard time when I asked her to let me stay home again, just asked was I cutting any tests or quizzes.

"Nah."

"Okay, but if you're staying home, you're staying home."

I offered her my keys.

She looked at them for half a minute, then said, "Just give me your word."

After she left for work, I got myself a Coke and went up in the attic.

The attic was where we kept a lotta shit. Lucky for me, Ma was pretty organized. Everything was in boxes marked on the outside with what was inside. Like "camping stuff" and "Christmas stuff" and "Jimmy's old toys." Things we never used were behind the shit we used once in a while, so I had to move a lot of boxes to find any that might hold Ma's old letters or diaries. I found a box marked "Billy's things" and dragged it under the light. There wasn't much in it—a folded flag, a Swiss army knife, an old manila envelope, a chain with dog tags with the name WILLIAM WILDING, B+, and a number that must've been his army ID number. There was a framed picture of Ma and Billy, taken in a city. They looked happy. He was all cool in his army uniform; she was in a dress. Where they were was warm but windy. Ma was wearing a hat and gloves, holding her hat on with one hand and a bunch of flowers with the other. Her skirt was flapping up, showing her legs. That had to be their wedding picture.

Another, smaller picture in the box was Ma between Billy and a guy I didn't recognize. It must've been taken the same day as their wedding, 'cause Ma and Billy were wearing the same clothes.

The manila envelope was full of pictures of people I didn't recognize, including the mystery guy from the wedding, plus older people, a few kids, and a black and white dog. I put them all back in the envelope and put everything but the knife back in the box. Billy was my birth dad so I guess that gave me as much right to his knife as anyone.

I hit the jackpot with the box marked "Rhiann's stuff." Beside the big bundle of letters addressed to Rhiann Reilly and Mrs. Billy Wilding, there were yearbooks and pictures and school stuff—programs, posters, etcetera.

Billy's letters were mostly bullshit, him telling Ma about the army—basic training was like the summer camp from Hell, AIT (whatever that is) was more interesting but it seemed like "the NCOs" were trying to scare them all into going AWOL. One of the letters said, "Dear Rhi, If you see Smoke, tell him that book he gave me was as advertised. I'm passing it around to the other guys in my platoon." Another letter, in a envelope postmarked May 18, 1969, said, "Dear Rhi, I may be home before you get this. My CO gave me a three-day pass to come to Mrs. Johnson's funeral. I told him she was my aunt. That's not too far from the truth since her son and me are blood brothers. Give Steve and Smoke a hug for me. Love, Billy."

I didn't read all the other letters—later for that. Ma would be home from work soon and I didn't want to get caught snooping. I bundled them back up and dug deeper into the box.

I found a marriage certificate for William Wilding and Rhiann Reilly. It was dated September 10, 1969. I was born on February 7, 1970. I'm no wiz at biology, but I know it takes more than five months to make a baby. So, I must've got my start when my dad came home for Mrs. Johnson's funeral.

John

Jimmy Fahey may only have known how to change oil, but the kid knew how to do it well. After letting him service my Jeep, I watched while he changed the oil in a customer's car. He worked slowly but methodically, apologizing profusely for not being faster. "Good is better than fast," I told him, echoing my old boss. He'd pick up speed as the job became autonomic and he got bored paying one-hundred-percent attention.

I finished the carburetor I'd been rebuilding and reinstalled it. Jimmy watched me adjust and test it, then check everything else under the hood. He went along on the test drive, asking pretty intelligent questions: Did I test-drive everything? How could I tell if something was wrong? What would I do if it broke down during the test?

"Do you always ask so many questions?"

"My dad says—*said*—it's the quickest way to find

things out."

"Smart man, your dad." The kid had nice manners, too, although I didn't point *that* out. "What time do you have to be home for dinner?"

"We usually eat around six-thirty."

"So we have time to tune that monster up." I pointed at his car, parked just outside the service door.

His eyes widened. "Don't we need parts?"

I indicated an auto parts box on the tool bench. "In the box."

He looked suspicious. "This is gonna cost me?"

"At least four more oil changes."

"Deal."

"Pull her in here, then. Let's get started."

With new wires, plugs, and points, a carburetor adjustment, and a small change in the timing, the kid's old Chevy ran like new. He seemed as happy as a five-year-old at Christmas. And we were done by six.

"When do you want me to do those oil changes?" he asked.

"You busy Saturday?"

"No. Can I bring my friend Finn?"

"If you promise you won't horse around."

"Swear to God."

Saturday, he showed up alone—his friend apparently had another engagement.

Jimmy changed the oil in three customers' cars, swept the shop, sorted the scrap metal from the reusable parts, took out the trash, and made a McDonald's run.

At the end of the day, I offered him a part-time job.

Jimmy

I was a couple blocks from home, coming from my new job, when red lights flashing in my rearview almost gave me a heart attack. I knew better than to hit the brakes—might as well sign a confession. I took my foot off the gas and put on my turn signal.

I pulled over and put the car in park. I watched in my side mirror as the sheriff's police cruiser stopped behind me. The deputy took his time getting out—must be checking my license plate with his dispatcher. He was as tall as my dad, but his gut hung out over his duty belt. He had on those mirror sunglasses the state troopers wear to look cool. They made this guy look sneaky. He was all red from too much sun and, as he walked up to the car, he was chewing gum with his mouth open. It made me think of a steer chewing its cud. The deputy spit his gum on the road and stood by my door with his fist on his gun and a thumb hooked under his belt.

Dumb. I'd seen Dad make traffic stops. He always kept his hands in front of him, in case he needed to move them in a hurry.

I rolled down the window and put my hands on the steering wheel.

The deputy looked familiar, but I couldn't place him. He said, "You know why I pulled you over?"

"No, sir."

"How fast were you goin'?"

"To be honest, I wasn't paying attention." A lie—I'd been twenty-five over, but I wasn't gonna tell *him* that.

"Ah-huhn."

Dad taught me to think of how a cop would see things: "You don't want anything you do to be misunderstood—might get you shot."

I kept my hands on the wheel till the cop said, "See your license?"

"It's in my wallet. In my back pocket."

"Get it out."

I did and handed it to him.

He looked at it. "You're Mickey Fahey's kid."

"Yes, sir."

"Sorry about your dad. He was my best friend."

Not! I thought, but I didn't say so.

"I'm Rory Sinter, by the way." He held out his hand.

What could I do? I shook it.

He said, "How's your ma holdin' up?"

"Okay, I guess."

"Hasn't been anybody hangin' around, botherin' her, has there?"

"No. Why would they? I mean, why'd anyone bother her?"

"'Cause she's a good-lookin' woman with no man to take care of her."

Dad always said be polite if you're pulled over. If it's a bogus stop, you can get a lawyer and fight it later. I had to fight myself to keep from saying, "Bullshit!" What I *did* say was, "She can take care of herself. And she's got me."

"An' I'm sure that makes her safe."

How stupid did he think I was? Not stupid enough to

disagree or argue.

He handed my license back. "I ain't gonna give Mickey's kid a ticket. But watch yourself, ya hear?"

I just said, "Yes, sir. Thanks."

I watched him in my rearview as he shut off his Mars lights and drove away.

Rhiann

Sunday morning, Jimmy and I went to church, then he went to "hang" with Finn. I took my newspaper out to read on the front porch. The day was brilliant, with jet trails scrawled across the sky like chalk lines on a pale blue slate. The grass was green enough to hurt your eyes. Snowdrift crabs along the parkway bloomed like banks of clouds fallen over neon-yellow dandelions and blood-red tulips.

Around eleven A.M., my new neighbor got out his lawn tractor and started cutting his grass. He was wearing Levi's, a navy T-shirt, and a straw cowboy hat like the landscapers wear. It was warm. Soaked with sweat, his shirt clung to his thin frame, making him look frail and undernourished. He drove as if he wanted to get done quickly.

Watching him made me feel hot and thirsty, and I went inside for something cool and wet.

John had finished his lawn by the time I came back out, with a plate of chocolate chip cookies and glasses of lemonade.

I waved him over.

He drove the tractor to the edge of my drive and shut the engine off. "As long as I have this out would you like me to cut your grass?"

"No, thanks. My husband never liked us to mow on Sunday. I'll get it tomorrow after work."

He nodded.

"Would you like something to drink?"

He accepted lemonade and a cookie and said, "I hope you don't mind that I offered your son a job?"

The phrase "better to ask forgiveness than permission" came to mind but I hid my annoyance. "Doing what?"

"Working on cars. He brought his Chevy in for a tune-up. He's working off the parts. But he's a natural. I'd like to keep him on."

"Where?"

"Black's Automotive."

"You're the manager?"

"The owner. I bought Black out when he retired to Florida last year."

I wondered why Jimmy hadn't told me about his car. He'd been sullen and secretive since Mickey died. Changed. Maybe he'd just turned into a teenager.

I hoped.

"Your son's a credit to his parents," John was saying.

I wondered what sort of influence he'd be. I'd have to ask around about him. Meanwhile, if Jimmy were kept busy…

"To my husband."

He nodded. "How'd you meet?"

"When he came back from Vietnam, he used to eat at the restaurant where I worked, and he seemed so sad I'd try to cheer him up. We got to be friends."

I wondered why I was telling this to a virtual stranger.

Maybe because he seemed as lonely and alone as Mickey had been when he came home from Nam. And John was a good listener.

A meadowlark staked his claim to the yard with song. We sat and sipped our lemonade, enjoying the scent of fresh-cut grass. What I *didn't* tell him was that when the army reclassified Billy as KIA, and I became a widow, Mickey had started courting me. And sometimes, when I couldn't get a sitter and had to bring Jimmy to work with me, Mickey played with him and kept him quiet when things got busy. And when Mickey finally told me that he loved me, and asked me to marry him, I had said yes.

I didn't want to keep thinking about Mickey; I'd start crying again. So I finished my lemonade and said, "How 'bout you? Any family?"

John shook his head. "My parents are dead. And I was an only child."

"No wife?"

He shook his head again.

"Have you always been a mechanic?"

"No, but it's a living. I like running the shop better." He helped himself to another cookie. "What do you do?"

"I run a shop, too. I'm girl Friday for a trucking company."

"You happy there?"

"Most of the time."

He nodded, then drained his glass and put it down. "Thanks."

I had a feeling that I'd lived this moment before. Déjà vu. The feeling passed. John was different from the men in my life—more reserved, maybe more thoughtful.

He stood up, pulled his glasses back over his eyes and replaced his hat, then restarted his mower and drove it away.

John

Jimmy was using his pocketknife to scrape the carbon off a spark plug one afternoon, when the knife slipped and dropped and went skittering across the floor. It came to rest against the wheel of my toolbox. I picked it up—an old Swiss army knife—and handed it back.

"Thanks," he said.

"It looks like it has a lot of years on it."

"It belonged to my birth father. The army returned it with his stuff after he died." He said it matter-of-factly, without the emotion he'd tried so hard to suppress when he told me about Mickey Fahey's death.

I pretended not to notice, pretended I didn't know the pain his birth father's death must've caused his friends and family.

"Every guy had one when I was a kid," I said. "My mother gave me one for Christmas when I was twelve."

"You still have it?"

"Nah. Haven't seen it in a donkey's age."

He nodded, put the knife in his pocket, and went back to work.

Jimmy

Two weeks before school let out, I had the sports section of the paper spread out on the kitchen island while Ma was getting dinner. She had out her cutting board, the big wooden salad bowl, and veggies—carrots, tomatoes, cucumbers, and a head of lettuce. She started tearing the lettuce into the bowl.

I folded up the paper and said, "Ma, were you ever a hippie?"

She sorta froze for a minute, then said, "Define 'hippie'."

"You know, like in the movie *Hair*. Did you burn your bra or draft card?"

"Girls didn't have draft cards. And burning my bra would make as much sense as taking the springs and shocks off my car."

"Well, did you go to love-ins?"

She gave me her don't-be-a-smart-ass look.

"How 'bout concerts?"

"A few."

"With Billy?"

"Ye-es."

Ma always told the truth or said, "None of your business," so I knew she wasn't lying. But the way she said "yes" made me wonder if she was telling the whole truth.

"Ever smoke pot?" I asked.

"I plead the fifth."

I laughed. "Protest marches?"

"No. I didn't know what there was to protest before Billy enlisted. Afterwards, I would've felt disloyal."

"You never told me he enlisted."

"You never asked!" We said it together; it was a family joke. We both laughed, then went quiet because it reminded us of Dad.

"Why'd he enlist?" I asked after a while. I was a little afraid my birth father would turn out to be one of those gung-ho GI Joe types.

"To spite his father," Ma said. "Or maybe just to get away from him. He lied about his age so he could sign up when he was seventeen."

"How come you never told me any of this before?" I pointed my finger at her. "Don't say 'cause I never asked."

She thought a minute. "Your birth father loved me and gave me the greatest gift a man could give a woman—you. But it makes me sad to think he isn't coming back, and that he'll never know his son. So I tend not to think of him too often.

"Anyway, we were both happy with your dad, so why bring up the past?"

"But don't I have any Wilding relatives?"

"Yes."

"Well?"

"They always hated me. And after Billy was reclassified KIA, Mrs. Wilding tried to have me declared an unfit mother."

Ma grabbed a carrot and started to chop it up like she was really pissed at it.

"But she didn't," I said. "Succeed, I mean."

"Only because your dad got me a killer lawyer. I haven't spoken to any of the Wildings in fifteen years." She put down the knife and scooped the carrots into the big salad bowl.

"Do you think they hate me, too?"

"I don't see how they could. They don't know you."

"Tell me about them."

"Billy's parents had money. They lived in the best neighborhood, went to the right church, knew the people in town who 'counted.' They had two sons—Billy and his older brother, Bobby.

"Bobby was a football player and a bully.

"Billy was a sweetheart. He hung out with me and my cousin, and another guy his parents didn't approve of. We were married—Billy and I—when he came home on leave, just before he was sent to Vietnam."

I got the feeling there was a whole lot to the story that Ma wouldn't tell me, even if I pushed. It made me more curious than ever, but I didn't ask. There was always the stuff in the attic. And I had all summer to snoop.

Rhiann

There are people like Mickey who light up a room when they come into it, who make you feel good just by showing up. And others—*perfect examples of "what's the use?"*—who make you feel depressed. Rory Sinter was one of the others.

It was a beautiful mid-May afternoon. I was weeding around my roses when he pulled his cruiser down the drive and stopped next to where I was working. He got out and left the motor running. I couldn't bring myself to say, "Good afternoon." I said, "Rory."

He leaned his back against the side of the car and crossed his arms. Crossed one ankle over the other, too.

Stupid. He'd trip himself if he had to move fast—Mickey'd taught me that. But that was Rory.

I kept pulling weeds. The soil was just damp enough to let go of the roots, and I was making headway against the dandelions and creeping charlie.

Rory'd positioned himself with the afternoon sun behind him. He wasn't considerate enough to block the light with his shadow, so I had to squint to look up at him.

He said, "How's things?"

"Okay." I wondered if he'd timed his visit to when I'd be close enough to the driveway so he could talk to me without having to go far from his car. Was he smart enough to plan that carefully? I didn't have to wonder what he wanted—he kept licking his lips.

I picked up my trowel and stabbed it in the ground next to a huge dandelion. I wiggled the tool, then tugged on the weed until its huge root broke free. I tossed it on the weed pile and sat back on my heels in Rory's shade.

"This a social call?"

His face was beaded with sweat. It wasn't hot; Rory was just fat. Before he answered, he took off his Smoky-bear hat and wiped the sweat from his face with his sleeve.

"Could say that," he told me, finally.

I waited.

"Might wanna tell that son of yours to ease up on the gas."

"You caught him speeding?"

"Clocked him doing sixty in a thirty-five."

"And what did you do about it?"

"Beg pardon?"

"You heard me."

"I ain't gonna give Mickey Fahey's kid a ticket."

I waited.

"I give him a warnin'."

"Next time, give him a ticket."

He blinked. Slowly. "You *want* me to give your kid a ticket?"

"If he breaks the law. Isn't that your job?"

"Yeah." He shook his head as if I was a hopeless case and pushed off from the cruiser. He'd opened the door and was about to put a foot in when he stopped and turned around. "Almost forgot."

I waited.

"Sheriff cleaned out Mickey's locker." A locker the sheriff let him use when he was working out of Rory's substation on the Joint Police Task Force. "He's got some of Mickey's things, 'cludin' his backup gun. I could run 'em by if you want."

"Thanks anyway. I have to talk to the sheriff. I'll pick them up."

"Suit yourself. You got a firearms card?"

"I do."

He nodded. He got into the cruiser and put on his mirror sunglasses. He stared at me for quite a long time before he put the car into gear and backed away.

As soon as he moved, I could see that John Devlin had pulled into his own drive and parked his Jeep parallel to Rory's car. John stood next to the Jeep, watching Rory pull away.

John's expression gave no hint of what he was thinking, but I had that feeling again of déjà vu.

When the deputy finally disappeared, John noticed me. He smiled and nodded, then went in his house.

John

Fathers make all the difference in a man's life. Good or bad. I know. Mine was the worst. Which is why Horace Black made such an impression on me. He never had any children of his own, but he fostered several generations of young men. His garage was a magnet for motor heads. Black let them hang around, and gave them work or advice—mechanical and philosophical—as long as they behaved. He had a way of making you want to impress him, and do better than you had. He never passed up the chance to put in a word on the evils of smoking or drugs or unsafe sex. In fact he kept a box of Trojans in his toolbox and let it be known that they were necessary and free.

I was beyond boyhood when I came to Black's but sorely in need of a father. And he obliged. He listened to me—even when I wasn't talking. He gave me work, encouragement, and praise. He taught me to channel anger into hard work, and passion into productivity. His patience and affection neutralized the rage eating like acid at my insides. He gave me choices—for the first time in my life.

So when he retired and sold his shop to me, I felt I owed him my soul. "How can I repay—?"

He held his hand up to stop me. "You don't repay love, John. Just do well. And pass it on."

I don't have all Black's gifts, but I've continued some of his traditions. I let kids hang around the shop. I don't let them smoke or horse around. I listen. I give advice when asked. And keep a box of Trojans in my Jeep. I encourage them to "Take a few for your glovebox because the condom in your wallet is sure to be worn out before it's unwrapped."

All of which is why when Jimmy Fahey confided that he'd been adopted, I didn't change the subject.

"Did you just find that out?" I asked.

"No. I've always known."

"So, why is it an issue now?" I knew the answer. A loved one's death can bring back earlier, unresolved losses. But he needed to figure that out on his own.

"Who says it's an issue?" he demanded.

"You brought it up."

He thought about that for a few minutes, then said, "I want to learn more about my birth father's family, but Ma won't talk about them."

"Did she say why?"

"Yeah. She says she's got her reasons, but she won't give me details. Or about my birth father, either."

"Maybe it's too painful."

"That's what *she* said."

"So what's the problem?"

It took a while for him to get it out. "I had an argument with my dad just before he was killed. I can't even remember what about. I *do* remember saying, 'You're just jealous because you're not my real father.' He looked like I sucker punched him, but I was too pissed off to say 'I'm sorry.'"

I said, "Your real father's the one who raised you, cheered at Little League games, sat in the ER when you broke something, went to PTA meetings at your school, and taught you how to throw a curve ball and change your oil."

"I know. I just wish I would've told him. And that I loved him."

"Do you believe in heaven?"

"I guess so."

"Then tell him. If there's a hereafter, he'll know. If there's not, *you'll* still know."

"I *still* need to know about my birth father."

"You might want to be careful. Remember what happened to Oedipus."

"Who's Oedipus?"

"Long story. And we've got a job to finish. Next time you're at the library, look him up."

Jimmy

I spent a lotta time in the attic the next couple days, reading Billy's letters. I felt like I was getting to know him pretty well. He had neat handwriting and a great sense of humor. He didn't get along with his family, but he loved my ma. I also learned that Billy grew up in Greenville with a couple of guys named Steve and Smoke that he loved "better than brothers," and that army life switched off between scary and boring as hell.

I went to the library with Finn, and he helped me find the Wildings' address and phone number. "What are you gonna do with this?" he asked.

"Reach out and touch someone."

"What if they won't talk to you?" I'd told him what Ma said about not talking to the Wildings for fifteen years. "Maybe you should write to them first."

"Nah. Dad always said it's harder for people to turn you down in person."

We looked up Oedipus, too.

"John's crazy," I told him. "This doesn't have anything to do with me. I'm not a orphan and my birth father died before I was even born."

"Yeah, an' you'd never even think about marrying your—Yech!"

One Friday after school, I gassed up my car and left a note for Ma: "Going to stay with a friend for the weekend.Love, J."

It took me an hour and a half to get to Greenville, even though it's only fifty miles, because I didn't know where I was going.

When I topped off at a Shell station outside town, a guy gave me directions: "On the corner of Elm and Main, across from the park. Big sucker. White. Can't miss it."

Rhiann

Our house rule has always been, if you're going to be away, leave a note to say where. So Friday afternoon, I wasn't surprised to find a message from Jimmy: "Ma, going to stay with a friend for the weekend. Love, J."

What friend? Where? Obviously he didn't want me to know so I couldn't veto his plans.

I called his buddy, Finn, and got the answering machine. I hung up and called Finn's mother. She put Finn right on the line.

He said, "Hello," as if he knew he was in trouble.

"Finn, where's Jimmy?"

"I really don't know, Mrs. F."

"Finn, you're old enough to be charged with aiding a runaway." I didn't know if there *was* such a charge, but I knew how to *sound* like there was. And a felony at that.

"Honest," Finn said, "he didn't tell me. He *did* look up his grandparents' address in Greenville."

"If you hear from him, tell him to call home or I'll have to report him missing."

That was a problem. We lived in an unincorporated area. I'd have to call the sheriff's police to make a report. Which meant Rory Sinter would probably get involved.

I hadn't talked to my cousin Steve in years, but I was desperate. I dialed the number from memory. After a moment I heard, "We're sorry. The number that you dialed has been disconnected."

John Devlin got home about five-fifteen and I was knocking on his front door two minutes later.

He seemed surprised. "Oh. Hello." He started to back up, to invite me in, but I was nearly frantic and a bit abrupt.

"Have you seen Jimmy? Did he work today?"

He shook his head. "He asked for the weekend off. He didn't say why. Things were slow, so I said sure. What's wrong?"

He seemed alarmed. Reflecting my own upset?

I realized I must be overreacting and took a deep breath. "Probably nothing." I handed him the note.

He read it and said, "I take it this is something new?"

I nodded.

"Well, he's what? Seventeen? This isn't unusual for a kid his age."

"I know. It's just—He was curious about his natural father's family. And I wasn't too…"

"Forthcoming?"

"Yes. And he may have gone to Greenville to find out about them for himself."

"Are they dangerous?"

I thought about that. Billy's brother was a bully, but I doubted he'd be violent towards my son. "Probably not."

"Then he'll be all right. He's got good instincts. He'll satisfy his curiosity and be back."

I must have still seemed worried because he added, "I could go to Greenville and look for him."

"No. Thanks anyway. I'm sure you're right. I'll wait. I'm sure he'll call."

Jimmy

The Wilding house was across one street from a park and across another from a restaurant, catty-corner to an insurance agency. The house was really cool—a big old two-story job with a round tower like a castle, and shingles—up under the roof—that looked like fish scales. A roofed-over porch ran all around the front and sides. The door was opened by an old lady dressed like she was goin' to church.

I told her who I was.

"I can't talk to you," she told me and closed the door in my face.

"Why?" I yelled. She didn't answer. I pounded on the door, but it stayed shut.

I hadn't expected that. I felt hurt, but I was curious. It couldn't be cause she hated me. She didn't know me. I wondered what was I gonna do next. I had a whole weekend that I'd been gonna spend getting to know my grandparents, but now…

As I walked back to the car, I spotted a guy sitting on the split-rail fence that surrounds the park. Watching me. He was an old guy—old as my ma, at least, and he had brown, curly hair long enough to hang over his collar. He was wearing a Cubs cap, a T-shirt that said, BEEN THERE/ SHIT HAPPENED, painters' pants, and tan work boots. A beat-up ten-speed leaned against the fence.

When he didn't look away, I checked to see what could be so interesting. Nobody and nothing around but me and my Chevy. I put my hands up like *"What!?"* He kept staring. Finally, I crossed the street and walked right up to him and said it. "What?!"

He slid off the fence. "You're not from around here, but you look familiar."

"Bet you say that to all the boys."

"No! Oh, no. I got my faults but that's not—You got business with the Wildings?"

"Who wants to know?"

"Steve Reilly."

Was I supposed to know him? I shrugged.

"Look," he said. "This is a small town. We got nothing to do but sit around and watch the grass grow. New kid comes to town—or stops to visit the Wildings, it's news."

"They're my grandparents."

"No lie! Let's see. Bobby's kids are all accounted for. And he doesn't have the imagination to have any woods colts. That must make you Rhiann and Billy's kid."

"You know my mom?"

"She's my cousin."

"She never told me—"

"She wouldn't. I'm the black sheep of the family. We used to be really tight when we were your age. But once she got married and had a kid she got religion."

I was skeptical. It sounded too much like a line some chicken hawk would use.

I musta looked it 'cause Steve said, "Look, you're smart to be careful. But call your mom—" He pointed across the street, to a pay phone outside the restaurant. "You were going to do that anyway to tell her you got here safe. She'll vouch for me."

I shook my head.

As if he read my mind, Steve said, "You didn't tell your mom you were coming, did you? You run away?"

"No-oo."

Steve nodded like, "yeah, sure," and pulled some coins from his pocket. "What's her number?"

I shook my head again.

"Hey, it's call your mom or I call the cops and report a runaway."

"Okay. Okay." I gave him Ma's work number.

Steve cut across the corner and dropped a quarter in the phone. He punched in the number and asked whoever answered for Mrs. Wilding.

"Fahey," I told him. "I thought you know my ma."

"Yeah, yeah. I forgot. She married the cop." To the phone, he said, "Sorry. I meant Mrs. Fahey." He listened for a minute, said, "Yeah, thanks," and hung up. "She's gone home," he told me. "What's your home number?"

I told him.

As he dialed it, he said, "Where're you staying?"

"You got a Y in town?"

"No. You're staying with me." He held up a finger—one minute. "Rhiann? It's Steve. You missing a kid? Yeah, don't worry. He's with me."

It took both of us pleading to get Ma to let me stay. She made me promise to be home early enough to get ready for school on Monday. And not to get in the car if Steve was driving.

By the time we hung up, I remembered where I heard the name Steve before. "You were that friend of Billy's when he was a kid."

"Your mom tell you about us?"

"No. Billy did."

"He died before you were born."

"Yeah, but he wrote home a lot. From all the letters, I'd say he didn't have much to do in the army but write."

"At least not that he could write your ma about."

Steve lived in a house that was sorta the opposite of Wildings'. Eighteen-nineteen Killdeer Lane was a little brown ranch—no porch, so surrounded by trees and bushes you could hardly see it from the street. Less grass to mow,

Steve explained as he took his bike outta my trunk. He left the bike by the front door.

Inside, the wall across from the door was covered with pictures, including the one of Ma and Billy and the mystery guy—who I now recognized was Steve. And Steve pointed out his parents, and Ma's—who I knew from visiting them in Florida.

In the living room, there were more pictures of Ma, Billy, and Steve, with another kid their age.

"Who's this guy?" I asked.

"Tommy Johnson. Nobody called him that, though. After the sixth grade, we called him Smoke."

"Why?"

"He used to introduce himself to newcomers by holding out his Marlboro box and saying, 'Smoke?' If they took one, he'd whip out his Zippo and light it for them. Then he'd wait until they took a drag before asking their name. Usually they'd end up coughing up a lung, and the rest of us would bust a gut laughing."

"Where'd you meet this guy?"

"We lived in Greenville all our lives—Smoke and Billy and me. The three of us hung out together forever—two musketeers and D'Artagnan. Smoke was D'Artagnan. He was only six months older than Billy, but he had a lifetime more years on him. He was always kidding around, but I could tell he was a sad clown, trying hardest to cheer himself up." Steve took a high school yearbook off a shelf under the TV. It looked like the same book Ma had in her box in the attic. Steve flipped it open to a picture of Smoke. He was kinda husky, with a blond crew cut and a "make-my-day" stare.

"He had a thing for trouble," Steve said. "If he wasn't causing it, he was fanning the flames. Guys used to say, 'Where there's fire, there's Smoke.' When the law showed up, he'd disappear—just like smoke." Steve laughed. "Some guy once said, 'Smoke, that's a nigger name, ain't it?' Smoke just gave him a evil little smile and said, 'Want to go outside and discuss it?' The guy suddenly remembered he had an appointment."

"My ma grew up with you guys?"

"She moved to Greenville the summer after fifth grade, when her folks bought the house next door to this one. Our dads were brothers, and we were both only children. My folks wanted me to be her older brother, but I wasn't into girls, specially relatives, so I spent the whole summer avoiding her. Smoke and Billy first met her when she started in the sixth grade. The three of us guys were always up for teasing. Smoke had caught a green frog on the way to school that day. He carried it into the building in his jacket pocket, planning to put it in the teacher's desk drawer. Until he spotted Rhiann in the hall before first period. I think it was love at first sight, but he wouldn't have admitted it to save his balls. Anyway, when he saw her, he hit my arm and said, 'Hey, a new girl.'

"'That's just my cousin.'

"'No shit! She's cute.'

"She had on a sleeveless red dress with a kind of a curved neckline—" Steve made a big U across his chest with his finger.

"I just shook my head. Smoke took the frog out of his pocket and sort of sauntered up to her, then grabbed the front of her dress and dropped the frog down it. We all waited for the screams."

He grinned. "Didn't happen. Rhiann reached into her dress and pulled out the frog. She marched up to Smoke, who was too surprised to run. She grabbed his belt buckle and pulled it toward her, then shoved the frog down his pants.

"It was the first time anyone ever got anything back on him. But he recovered fast. He reached in his pants and pulled the frog out. He held it up like he was looking it in the eye. 'Lucky frog,' he said. 'You've been to no man's land and paradise and lived to tell about it.'

"Of course, everybody started to laugh.

"Except Rhiann. She got the last laugh. She got right in Smoke's face and said—loud enough for everyone to hear, 'Keep your filthy frogs to yourself.'

"She made him laugh. He took it on himself to be her older brother and made us let her in the club. We were the four musketeers after that."

"Where's Smoke now?" I asked.

"MIA. He ran away. Billy disappeared in Vietnam. I've been sort of AWOL from life the last fifteen years. I guess we all went missing one way or another."

Jimmy

Steve took me around town and pointed out the high school, the swimming pool, and the Dairy Queen where he used to hang out with Rhiann, Billy, and Smoke in "the good old days."

"I s'pose I oughta feed you," he said, after a while.

"You hungry?"

"Don't you gotta be to work pretty soon?"

"Yeah. You think if I gave you my house key you could amuse yourself?"

"Sure. What's there to do around here?"

"Well, we got a bowling alley, a theater, an' a video arcade."

"That ought to keep me busy for an hour or two."

"Oh, and a public library."

"Cool! I could do my homework."

"Don't be a smart-ass."

I dropped Steve off at Hannigan's, where he worked as a bartender. After driving all the way from Overlook, I didn't feel much like sitting another two hours in a movie. That narrowed it down to bowling, the video arcade, or the library. I was on my way to check out the arcade when I spied the golden arches. Friday night Mickey D's ought to be hopping. I parked and went inside.

Judging by the people—a few truckers, families, and groups of kids—Greenville wasn't a whole lot different than Overlook. I like people-watching, so I got a Quarter Pounder, large fries, and a Coke and sat down where I could keep an eye on things.

I was almost finished when I spotted the *cutest* girl I'd ever seen, a blonde a head shorter than me. She was in line with another girl, and they were really into their conversation, so I got to stare without pissing them off. I wasn't the only one who noticed. These three guys in Greenville starter jackets got in line behind them and started crowding them and mouthing off. The girls ignored them at first—until one of the guys grabbed the blonde's purse and held it over his head.

"Hey, *jerk!*" She jumped up trying to grab the purse.

The guy just turned around, keeping it out of her reach. His buddies thought it was *hilarious*.

I looked around. Everybody was watching, no one offering to help.

I wondered if the bully's pals would stand behind him if I butted in. I didn't wonder long. Dad always said bullies'll back off if you stand up to them. So I did.

Stepping up behind him, I grabbed the purse. The blonde was standing off to the side, staring at me. I pretended to ignore her. I handed the purse to her girlfriend, who was closer, and stayed between the girlfriend and the creep so he couldn't take it back.

"Why don't you pick on someone your own size?" I asked him.

"Like you, asshole?" the bully said.

The two girls retreated to a safe distance.

"Mr. Fahey to you, butthead."

"Oooh. Tough guy!" Without warning, he threw what would've been a sucker punch if it had landed.

Dad had taught me what to do about stuff like that. I turned sideways and grabbed his fist as it flew by. Pivoting in the same direction he'd thrown the punch, I kept hold of his wrist and stepped forward. I got out of the way as he fell. He ended up facedown on the floor at the feet of the blonde.

She giggled.

Her friend pounded the air with her fist. "Yes!"

Everybody else stared.

The bully started to get up. His face went as red as a large fries holder.

Then the manager came charging out from behind the counter. "Get outta here! All a you!"

I smiled at the blonde and bowed.

She smiled back. Then she and her friend headed for the ladies' room.

The bully got up and started toward me, but the manager blocked his way. I went for the exit.

The bully yelled, "Hey, chicken!" after me.

I didn't even turn, just put my hand over my head and waved as I walked away. Once I was outside, I decided that the girls would be all right with the manager there. But with three against one, I might not do as well once the goons got away from him. I jumped in my car and burned rubber peeling out of the lot so everybody inside would know I'd left.

I tore up to the next corner and squealed my tires turning right. As soon as I was out of sight of McDonald's, I slowed down. I really wanted to see the blonde again. I went around the block like I was taking my driver's test. I crept up to Mickey D's entrance just as the goons screeched out the exit, turning the same way I had.

They never looked back, just took off like the Dukes of Hazard.

When the blonde and her friend came out of the restaurant, I was right in front of the door, leaning on the hood of my car.

"Evenin', ladies. Need a ride?"

The blonde giggled and elbowed her friend.

Her friend said, "We're not allowed to take rides from strangers."

"I'm Jimmy Fahey. And you are…?"

"Beth," the blonde said.

"Beth?" I circled my hand to encourage her to give me her whole name.

"Just Beth." She pointed at her girlfriend. "This is Stephanie."

I said, "Stephanie."

"Did you just move here?" Beth asked.

"I came to visit my grandparents." I let it go at that. No sense confusing her with the details.

"Where'd you learn kung fu?"

"That wasn't kung fu, just a little self-defense move my dad taught me."

"Pretty cool," Stephanie said.

I smiled. Out of the corner of my eye, I caught sight of the manager coming toward us. I said, "Now that I'm not a stranger, can I give you a lift?"

"We left our car at the library," Stephanie said.

The manager came out the door at a run.

I jumped to the passenger side and yanked the door open. "Get in. I'll drive you there."

They did. Beth first, I noticed.

I closed the door and held my hands up in front of the charging manager. "Just picking up my sister, sir."

That seemed to throw him. He stopped. He opened his mouth and closed it. "Which one's your sister?"

Stephanie looked the most like me, so I pointed to her.

The manager pointed at Beth. "Who's she?"

"My girlfriend."

He frowned, then said, "Get the hell outta here!"

"Yes sir."

"And don't come back!"

Stephanie did most of the talking. Beth navigated. I tried to keep my mind on my driving and my hands to myself. I still wasn't real familiar with Greenville, but it seemed to me we went a couple miles out of the way before we finally turned into the lot next to the big gray stone library.

I shut off the engine. Stephanie got out, still talking.

"Can I get your number?" I asked Beth.

She shook her head. "My dad'd kill me if I got a call from a boy."

"How old are you?"

She laughed again. I loved her laugh. "Sixteen."

Sweet! Jailbait! "An' I s'pose you've never been kissed? When're you gonna be seventeen?"

She smiled. "In September."

I could wait. "When can I see you again?"

"I'll be at the library next Friday night."

Rhiann

When I opened the door the next morning, John Devlin was on my porch. Behind him, in the yard, the leaves of the cotton-woods reflected light like bright green sequins. The morning was cloudless, the air still cool. A light breeze blew John's scent toward me—a faint, pleasant aftershave I couldn't name. John had on the navy blue T-shirt he usually wore to cut his grass. He looked too thin and a little sad until he smiled.

"Good morning," he said. "Did your son turn up?"

"He called. He went to visit relatives. He didn't tell me ahead of time because he was afraid I'd veto the plan."

"He's at that age."

"I know. But he's been so crazy since his father died I almost don't know him."

John nodded—sympathetically, I thought. There was something irritatingly familiar about him but…

I added, "You've been good for him."

"I guess I see in him the son I might have had."

"You never married?" I waited. I let silence draw him out.

"I had a girl, once, but I took off—left her in the lurch—so she married someone else. Just as well. She didn't need a felon for a husband."

The fear that passed through my mind must have shown on my face. I *hid* my anger. How *dare* he hire my son…

He added, "I guess you'll be afraid now."

"What were you convicted of?"

"Reckless homicide."

Homicide? This quiet, polite man? And reckless? "Reckless" suggested unfeeling or thoughtless or immature. Everything I'd seen of John was just the opposite.

"You don't seem reckless."

"Not anymore." He turned away.

"John."

He turned again to face me.

"I'm not afraid."

John

I hadn't been able to make bail, so I spent the weeks waiting for trial in the Cook County lockup. I had a lot of time to read—mostly paperbacks with pages missing. I didn't have money to pay a lawyer, so they assigned me a public defender.

The woman seemed too young to be responsible for people's lives, only a few years older than I. Thin and hyperactive with straight red hair and a bright orange sweater suit. She took her responsibility seriously. When I told her I was going to plead guilty, she said, "You're crazy."

I shrugged. "I killed a man." Not on purpose, but he was just as dead.

"That doesn't mean you have to ruin your life, too."

I didn't tell her my life was ruined already.

"I can plead this down to a misdemeanor charge," she told me. "With time served, you could be out in ten months—no felony record."

I was alive. I didn't deserve more than that. I felt as worthless as my old man always claimed I was. I just shook my head.

The courtroom was small and round, with a wooden bench, jury box, and tables. Spectators sat in three curved rows of wooden pews. All the wood didn't make up for the yellowed acoustical tiles, dingy off-white walls, or the lumpy linoleum floors that were shiny from numerous coats of wax. I was herded in from the holding cell and stood, as ordered, with my hands behind my back. Reckless homicide was a class three felony—five to ten years. They'd offered me the minimum for pleading guilty, not that I wouldn't have anyway. I was guilty.

The judge seemed bored. "You understand that if you plead guilty you won't be able to appeal?"

"Yes, sir."

The PD shook her head. Vigorously. Several times. Until the judge gave her an annoyed look. He spoke. The court reporter typed away on her machine. I stopped listening.

After a while, the sheriff's deputy tapped me on the shoulder, then herded me back to the holding cell.

Prison should have scared me but it didn't. By nineteen, I'd seen and lived through so much I wouldn't have broken a sweat if they'd marched me through the gates of hell. Which pretty much described Stateville.

I hadn't even heard of Dante when the bus pulled up to intake. But years later, reading the *Inferno* had been an epiphany. Everything about the maximum-security facility was hellish, from the annular architecture to the never-ending din of despairing souls.

Jimmy

Steve slept in Saturday—'till noon. I got up early and scrounged some breakfast—he had Cap'n Crunch! I watched cartoons for a while, then snooped around the house.

There was a family album on the coffee table. I studied the pictures. I recognized my mom and dad, and Billy Wilding, Steve, Grandma and Grandpa Reilly, and the guy Steve called Smoke. There were lots of people I didn't recognize, but most of the stuff you could figure out—like the Fourth of July, and parades, picnics, weddings, and Christmases. Ma and Billy and Smoke were in some of the pictures, but most of 'em must've been Steve's family.

When Steve got up, he seemed surprised to see me. Then it was like he remembered who I was.

He stretched and yawned and scratched his stomach. "What's for breakfast?"

I handed him the Cap'n Crunch box; he looked like he was gonna barf. "You could've at least made coffee."

"I would, only there was no coffee. And no filters. And I don't know where the stores are around here."

"C'mon," he said. "You're driving."

The Eat Well diner was kinda like Denny's—you could get breakfast any time. Which is what we did.

The waitress reminded me of Gramma Reilly—heavy and real cheerful. She had on a pink flowered dress and nurse's shoes with crew socks. Her apron had ruffles and big pockets. According to her badge, her name was Carol. As she came towards the table with a coffeepot and two mugs, Steve leaned over and whispered, "Don't tell her anything you don't want the whole town to know."

"Gotcha."

"Hi, Steve," Carol said. "Coffee?"

Steve said, "Yes, ma'am."

She put down the mugs and patted Steve on the back while she poured—like he was a kid. Then she looked from me to Steve and said, "Aren't you gonna introduce us?"

"Yeah. Sorry, Carol. This is my cousin Jimmy. Jimmy, Carol."

"Pleased to meet you." Carol held up the coffeepot. "How 'bout you?"

"Ah. No, thanks."

"What'll it be, then?"

"A Coke?"

She nodded. "You boys ready to order?"

Steve nodded and asked for eggs and sausage and pancakes and OJ and more coffee. Carol took a little notebook out of her pocket and wrote it all down. I asked for a burger. Deluxe. She wrote that down, too. Then she went in the back.

While she was gone, we stared at the other three people in the place—two cops and a lady who looked about a hundred. The old lady ignored us, just kept reading the newspaper. When the cops were finished eating, they got up and dropped money on the table. One of them headed for the men's room; the other headed our way.

"You stayin' outta trouble, boy?" he asked Steve.

"Sure thing, Sheriff."

The sheriff turned to me. "Who might you be?"

"I might be Steve's cousin Jimmy."

"Don't be a smart-ass."

"No, sir."

"And don't be followin' in your cousin's footsteps."

I didn't bother to answer; the sheriff didn't seem to notice. When his deputy came out of the can, they went away.

As soon as the door closed behind them, I asked Steve, "What was that about?"

"I haven't had a drink in three years—nobody around here's noticed. They still treat me like I'm just comin' off a drunk or headed into one.

"But they like me, so they're subtle about it."

Steve and I spent the rest of the day hanging out. We took in a movie, then bowled a few games. I suggested McDonald's for dinner, and Steve was a good sport about it, even though he didn't seem excited about Big Macs. I didn't see Beth or Stephanie anywhere. And I sure was keeping an eye out.

Later, I dropped Steve off at work, then went back to his house and watched TV until I fell asleep.

Steve rousted me early the next morning. He handed me a sport jacket that was too big and a tie that looked like a hand-me-down from his grandfather.

"What's this for?"

"We're goin' to church."

I didn't argue. I'd gone to church with my parents almost every Sunday of my life. We stopped at Dunkin' Donuts for some breakfast on the way.

The church was a big old gray stone job with a bell tower and stained-glass windows. It wasn't Catholic or Baptist, so I was worried I wouldn't know the prayers. Steve said not to worry, just do what everybody else did and say whatever I liked. He said us going was mostly just a social call. And anyway, you didn't need to go to church to pray.

We sat in the last pew, where you couldn't see anything but the ceiling and the back of people's heads. The service was long and the sermon was boring. Steve seemed to be bored, too. I didn't get the point.

Afterward, just outside the door, Steve stepped in front of a big overweight guy walking with his wife and two boys. The guy looked like an ex-football player; his wife looked scared of her own shadow.

"What do you want, Reilly?" the guy asked.

"I want to introduce you to your nephew."

"Who?" You'd've thought Steve was speaking Klingon.

Steve said, "This is Jimmy, Billy's kid. Jimmy, this is your uncle Bobby."

"No shit!" Bobby must've realized what he'd just said and where, 'cause he turned bright red. He looked around; nobody seemed to be paying attention. He stared at me. "You really Billy's kid?"

I nodded.

He offered me his hand. "Nice to meet you, kid. What brings you to town?"

I shook his hand and shrugged.

He didn't introduce me to his wife. When one of the

kids started whining, Bobby made a face. His wife grabbed both kids by their collars and hurried them toward the parking lot. Bobby watched them for a minute, then said, "You'll have to come by the house sometime and get acquainted with your cousins." He didn't mention a time frame. "Bring him by the house one day," he told Steve. Then he turned and walked away.

"Steve. What was that about?"

He grinned. "He's an asshole. Don't take it personal." He looked around. "Hope we do better with your grandparents."

Now I got it. I looked around, and sure enough, Mrs. Wilding was coming out of the church, between the minister and a skinny old man in a suit that fit him as well as Steve's jacket fit me. I waited till they were closer to say, "Good morning." I didn't know what to call them. "Grandma" and "Grandpa" seemed too personal, but "Mr. and Mrs. Wilding…"

She acted like I wasn't there. The old man seemed like nobody was there.

I stepped in front of my grandmother. "Why won't you talk to me?"

That got her. "Your mother threatened to have me jailed."

"That was a long time ago. Things've changed."

"I wish I had your confidence in that."

"You would if you knew my ma." I thought she looked surprised. Maybe she wasn't used to wiseass kids. I said, "Careful, you're smiling."

That did make her smile. She said, "You have your father's sense of humor."

"What was he like?"

"Didn't your mother tell you?"

"Yeah, but just her version."

"Come back next weekend and stay with me. I'll tell you."

"Sure. Thanks."

Sunday afternoon, I didn't want to leave, but I'd promised Ma I'd be home.

The highway between Greenville and home was nearly empty. I cranked the Chevy up to eighty. The wind pounded my ears. I had to turn the radio way up to hear it. In the forty-five minutes it took me to get home, I had a chance to think about the conversation I had with Steve before I left:

"My dad didn't like you much, did he?" I'd said.

"Mickey?"

"Yeah. *He's* my real dad."

Steve stared off into space for a minute. "Mickey always liked everyone. It was more like he didn't approve of me."

"Why?"

"Maybe 'cause I never made anything of myself."

I had the feeling there was more. I waited.

Steve said, "And there was your mother."

I raised my eyebrows.

"Mickey knew I loved her."

"Your cousin?"

He waved his hand at me like that didn't mean anything. "You got a girlfriend?"

I thought of Beth. "No one special." Yet. "Just some friends who're girls."

"Then you wouldn't understand. But someday you'll

meet *the one*. When it hits, you'll feel stupid whenever you get near her, and your hands and feet'll be too big. And your brain'll be warm Jell-O. You'll see.

"We all felt that way about Rhiann. She was Smoke's from the get-go. He pretended he didn't care, but that was just 'cause he didn't feel he deserved her.

"When he left, we had a clear field. I guess Billy wanted her more. He asked her first."

"Why do you s'pose my ma never told me any of this?"

"Was she happy with Mickey?"

"Well, ye-ah."

Steve shrugged. "Then why bring up the past?"

"How come you and my ma didn't keep in touch?"

"A couple reasons. It was too painful for me to make the effort, for one. And I think Mickey was uncomfortable having me around 'cause he knew how I feel about Rhiann."

"Still?"

"You never get over your first love, kid. Even if it's unrequited."

Rhiann

Tuesday morning, as rain slapped the window glass, I came awake in a flashback.

"Mornin', sunshine." Mickey lay propped on his elbows next to me, smiling. Clouds hid the sunrise beyond our window, so his face was lit only in silhouette.

"What are you doing?" I asked.

"Memorizing your face."

"You ought to have it down by now."

He smiled. "Don't want to forget any detail."

"In case you have to describe me to your sketch artist?" That was our inside joke. The state police sketch artist was a computer that turned out generic pictures of vague similarity to their subjects.

"In case you finally wise up and leave me."

I shook my head and grabbed the front of his T-shirt. "You'd be too hard to replace. All the good guys are taken." I tugged the shirt.

He shifted on top of me, keeping his weight suspended on his arms. He was quick and graceful for a man his size.

I pretended to struggle.

The first time I'd played the game, he'd stopped, horrified. Now, fifteen years later, he smiled and kissed me until I arched my body upward, inviting him inside.

"Oh, God!" I bit into my lip, trying to distract myself from the sudden awful emptiness the memory left me with. Withdrawal. His absence was almost as real, physically, as the weight his body had been on mine.

I threw the covers back and rolled off the bed to escape the void where his comforting bulk had lain. A void like a ghost. Not his ghost. If there'd been anything of his spirit left here, it would have been comforting, not like this.

I snatched clothes from my drawers and closet and

fled to the bathroom, hoping a hot shower would wash the ache away.

John

I knew at a glance that Jimmy'd met a girl. Before I even said hello, I detoured past my Jeep and got him a handful of Trojans.

"What are these for?" he demanded. Before I could answer, he figured it out and turned bright red. But he didn't refuse the condoms.

"Can I have next weekend off?" he asked. "Or at least next Friday?"

"That serious, huh?"

"Yeah."

"Congratulations."

That seemed to startle him. "I haven't really—I just met her."

"That's a start."

"But I don't even know how to talk to girls. I mean—*You* know what I mean."

"Yeah. I'm a *real expert* on women."

"What if she doesn't like me?"

"If you treat her right, how can she resist you?"

"What do you mean 'treat her right'?"

I laughed. "How did your dad act around your mother?"

His eyes widened. "But they were married."

"Not at first. Ask your mom. She can tell you how to treat a girl."

"Hey! I could ask my ma."

"Why don't you do that? Later. Meanwhile, why don't you change the oil in that Ford?"

"I could do that." He started toward the car then stopped. "Hey, you never answered my question."

"What question?"

"Can I have next weekend off?"

Rhiann

Friday afternoon there was another note from Jimmy: "Ma, Grandma Wilding invited me to spend the weekend with her. I'll be back Sunday nite. Love, J"

He'd been extra helpful all week—maybe making up for last weekend, maybe because Finn was wrapped up in his girlfriend and not available to "hang." It made me sad—my son growing up, getting a life away from me.

I changed into shorts and went to take my bad feelings out on the weeds in my garden. We'd had rain two days before, and the soil was crumbly soft. In no time, I had my wheelbarrow full of dandelions and creeping charley.

If I'd thought about it, I'd have known Rory would come back. I didn't think about him until his shadow fell across me.

"Afternoon, Rhiann."

I shivered. "Rory. What brings you today?"

"You didn't pick up Mickey's gun."

Fighting the urge to tell him "none of your business," I just stared.

He leaned sideways, moving his shade so the sun struck me in the face.

I sat back on my heels and reached my gimme cap from my gardening tote. "Is the sheriff planning to auction it off?"

"Just thought you might need it, bein' as how your new neighbor's a convicted felon."

I felt a sudden rage and stood up, stepping into his space. "And you know this how?"

"I ran a check on him for you. Did five years for killin' a man. They shoulda nailed him for DUI, too, but he lost so much blood the paramedics had to give 'im fluids. Brought his BAC down below the legal limit by the time they took a sample."

I felt like slapping him. Instead, I took a deep breath and said, "Why are you telling me this?"

"Just watchin' out for my best friend's widow."

"If I want help, I'll ask."

"Maybe you weren't list'nin'. Devlin's a convicted felon."

"He's done his time. And as long as he's not breaking any laws, he has a right to be left alone. So do I. Please go away."

"You taken leave of your senses?"

I didn't answer.

"Mickey must be spinnin' in his grave."

"Mickey was a Christian. He believed in redemption and forgiveness."

Rory laughed. "Yeah. Did ya hear me say Devlin killed a man?"

"Reckless homicide, wasn't it?"

"He told you! Well, he probably figured you'd find out."

"What was he, eighteen or nineteen at the time?"

"A leopard don't change his spots."

"The only spotted thing around here is your motive, Rory. Please leave."

"You're gonna regret it."

When John Devlin pulled into his drive an hour later, I was still furious at Rory. Which may have clouded my judgment.

John looked tired, almost old, as he got out of his Jeep—nothing like the felon Rory tried to make him out.

Then he smiled, and I wondered again if he were younger than his white hair suggested.

I stabbed my shovel into the earth and said, "John?"

Jimmy

It took me less than an hour to get to Greenville Friday afternoon. This time I knew where I was going—straight to Mickey D's. I looked around for the Greenville goons and, when I was sure the coast was clear, I went in and checked the plumbing. Then I got a large Coke and directions for a shorter route to the library.

The big old building had really big trees around the parking lot and really tall doors and windows. Stephanie's car wasn't in sight, so I parked in the shade and took my time finishing my Coke.

Inside, the place was kinda like a church—lots of old carved wood and stained-glass windows. But instead of Bible stories, the pictures looked like fairy tales. There were posters, too—actors like Michael J. Fox and Whoopi Goldberg telling people to READ.

An older lady was sitting on a tall stool behind the checkout desk. She looked up from the book she was reading and said, "May I help you?"

"Urn. I'm s'posed to meet someone here."

She smiled and nodded, then went back to her book.

John

I could tell by the way my neighbor was attacking the weeds that she was upset. Her skin glowed red, whether from anger or too much sun, I couldn't tell. Her shirt, damp with sweat, clung to her skin. She was beautiful!

She gave me an ambiguous smile when I got out of the Jeep, so I guessed she wasn't mad at me.

I smiled back, then started to get my stuff together.

She took a couple more whacks with her shovel, then drove it hard enough into the ground to stand it upright.

I started toward my house.

"John," she called after me.

I stopped and turned. "Yes?" I was ready to say yes to anything she asked.

She seemed startled, as if she'd forgotten that she'd spoken. I waited. Finally she said, "There's a potluck supper at the church tonight. You're welcome to join us."

Not exactly the invitation I'd dreamed of, but a start. "What can I bring?"

"They can always use milk or soda."

I nodded. "I'll drive?"

She seemed, suddenly, uncomfortable. "Maybe we'd better go in separate cars." Before I could feel hurt by that, she added, "Deputy Sinter was a friend of my husband's and he seems to feel it necessary to look out for Mickey's widow. He made a point to warn me about you."

I couldn't keep from smiling. "So you immediately decided to convert me."

She laughed, then sobered. "He can be a real jerk. I wouldn't want to give him an excuse to bother you."

"I see. You're protecting me from Deputy Sinter."

She smiled—a troubled smile it seemed to me. "I wouldn't put it quite like that."

"Who's going to protect *you*?"

"My husband was a *state* cop. That trumps the sheriff's police. If Rory actually makes trouble, I'll ask Mickey's old boss to set him straight." She smiled again. "I'm sorry. I should have said so first—that Rory will probably be there—I don't want to put you on the spot and—I'll understand if you want to change your mind." She sounded as though she'd be disappointed if I didn't come.

That and her smile were enough to convince me. "I'll be there."

Though I didn't say it, I knew that if Sinter became a problem she'd need someone to back her up until the state police arrived.

In which case, I was her man.

• • •

The church was an unassuming brick structure with a cross over the door formed by bricks set out half a width from the wall face. The parking lot was shaded by half-century-old elms and overgrown lilac bushes. I waited until Rhiann arrived. Then, carrying my galvanized tub filled with ice and pop cans, I followed her into the church basement and stopped just inside to watch her.

She could've been a model in her flowered dress. Her hair was pulled back, tied with a ribbon. She seemed to know everyone and greeted them with a hug and a dazzling smile. But when she thought no one was looking, a sad expression crossed her face like mist clouding the sun.

She noticed me standing with my offering and hurried over. "John, I'm so glad you came."

She showed me where to put the tub—on the end of a long table covered with a red-and-white checked oilcloth and laden with casseroles, salads, meat and cheese trays, and condiments. Then she insisted on introducing me around.

Surviving prison leaves you with a peculiar skill set, one tool of which is the ability to closely observe what's going on around you while seeming to attend to something else. So I was able to observe Rhiann while shaking hands with the Reverend and Mrs. Poplar.

The reverend and his wife watched Rhiann with concern, as if waiting to offer comfort at the first sign it was needed. And why not. Her husband was only three months in his grave.

I noticed two others watching her. Frank Farmer, the old man she introduced as her boss, eyed her with longing.

Deputy Sinter—out of uniform but no less officious than when we'd first met—leered at her when he thought no one was looking, especially the brassy woman with him whom I took to be his wife.

When Sinter saw me he flushed, and his jaw muscles knotted. I'd met men like him. In prison, they were guards or gang bosses. Bullies. You didn't want to give them trouble in front of witnesses—they couldn't stand to lose face. But you never wanted to let them back you down.

When Rhiann said, "Rory, you've met my new neighbor," she didn't smile.

Neither did he. He said, "Devlin."

"And this is Marie," Rhiann told me.

I gave her a friendly nod—though not too friendly. "Mrs. Sinter."

Sinter turned a shade darker. The expression "if looks could kill" crossed my mind.

Marie Sinter smiled. "Nice to meet you, Mr. Devlin." Her smile faded as she noticed her husband's reaction. She looked from him to me to Rhiann, clearly hoping for an explanation.

Ignoring Marie's confusion, Rhiann took my arm, saying, "Excuse us, Marie." To me she said, "John, you've got to meet Abel. He desperately needs help with his old car."

Before we retreated, I saw Sinter whisper something to his wife. Marie looked alarmed.

Sinter made a point to get me alone later. "I got my eye on you. You step outta line you'll be back in jail so fast you won't know what hit you."

I didn't bother to answer. I'd done five years—didn't

bother to apply for parole. So when I got out, I was a free man—or as free as you can be when you've killed someone.

Most people are willing to give you the benefit of the doubt, but there were always the Sinters...

Rhiann

After I introduced John around, I left him with Abel Smith who'd had problems with his Ford Taurus ever since he got it.

I knew inviting John was a mistake when I saw Rory Sinter working his way around the room, bending the ear of every man still speaking to him. When I saw him buttonhole Frank, I decided to try limiting the damage his malicious gossip might do. I started with the Poplars.

"John's had some trouble in his past. But whatever Rory's told you, John's trying to straighten his life out."

Reverend Poplar is a great preacher—he understands the world as well as the Word. He patted my arm. "Then it's a good thing you brought him to us." To his wife he said, "Come on, my dear," and led her toward where John was still talking to Abel.

Jimmy

"The library is closing."

I came awake in a panic. Where was I?

Greenville. The library.

Where was Beth?

The librarian didn't push me—maybe she saw how bummed I was—but I could tell she wanted to go home. So I said, "Thanks," and "Good night," and went out to sit in my car.

There was no sign of Beth or Stephanie or Stephanie's car. I finally gave up and went looking for Steve. I didn't find him. When I spotted the Greenville goons' car in the Mickey D's parking lot, I decided it was time to go to my grandmother's.

The Wilding house must've been the biggest one in Greenville. Big old elm trees shaded it, and there were tons of bushes along the drive out front. The porch wrapped all around and had a roof so, on rainy days, you could sit out and watch traffic splash by.

I climbed the front steps and knocked.

Mrs. Wilding opened the door herself. Again. She frowned, and—for a minute—I thought she was gonna repeal her invitation. Then she said, "Do you have a suitcase?"

Weird.

"Yes, ma'am."

She looked past me, at my Chevy—and her mouth formed a hard, straight line. I guess the car didn't meet her standards. Like I cared. But I was starting to wonder why I was here. The trip had been an excuse to see Beth again. Without Beth, it was nuts to put up with Mrs. Wilding. Ma would've called her rude. Maybe that was why they didn't get along.

Mrs. Wilding said, "You can park behind the house, next to the garage. Come to the back door and I'll let you in."

The back door opened onto the same big porch that surrounded the front of the house. Mrs. Wilding stood back to let me into the biggest kitchen I'd ever seen. I bet most hotels have smaller ones.

A little old black lady was sitting at the table, peeling potatoes. She was wearing a white uniform, an apron, and nurse's shoes.

"This is Rosa," Mrs. Wilding said. She told Rosa, "This is William's son, James."

Rosa looked surprised.

"Rosa was your father's nanny," Mrs. Wilding said. "Would've been yours."

"Master James," Rosa said. Softly.

"No," I said. "Just Jimmy."

Rosa threw a look at Mrs. Wilding. *She* didn't seem to be listening. She was walking around the room like she expected to find something out of place. Who knows what? The room looked like an ad in one of my ma's *House and Garden* magazines.

Rosa said, "Jimmy," very softly.

"And not master, Rosa," I added. "President Lincoln freed the slaves."

She chuckled. "You got your daddy's sense a humor. But you got to know master's an old-fashioned word. Means a young man's not old enough to be a mister."

I grinned; Rosa winked.

Mrs. Wilding said, "Come along, Will—Ah, James."

A Freudian slip! My dad told me about them. Cops use 'em to trip up criminals. I just said, "Yes, ma'am."

The house was like Dr. Who's Tardis—big as it was on the ouside, it seemed bigger inside. Mrs. Wilding led me through a huge dining room and even bigger front room. All the furniture was old-fashioned—dark wood, heavy. They looked to me like antiques. And like they didn't get used very much.

The room she called the library had twelve-foot ceilings and bookshelves that went all the way up and were full of books—lots of 'em with matching covers. I'm sure there were more than in the public library.

"Did you read all these?" I asked her.

She got a funny look on her face—like I'd caught her doing something she shouldn't. "Most of them. Not all."

I only own three books—*Catch-22, Catcher in the Rye*, and *Breakfast of Champions*—but I've read 'em all. At least twice.

We finally got to a huge staircase and I followed her up the steps.

She stopped at the top to get a breath, and I took the opportunity to ask, "Where's Grandpa?"

"Your grandfather is resting." She hesitated. "He's not well."

"What's the matter with him?"

She gave me a look—you know, "How rude"—that I ignored. Finally, she said, "He's losing his mind." She seemed almost ready to cry, but she didn't.

I said, "I'm sorry."

The staircase ended in a hallway that went right and

left. Each side ended at a really tall window. She turned left. "You've nothing to be sorry for. It's not your fault."

"Yes, ma'am."

She stopped and turned to face me. "Call me 'grandmother.' Please." I nodded. She said, "You *are* welcome here. Whatever your mother may've said."

"She didn't say anything."

"Good."

She turned and went farther down the hall, then opened one of the doors and went in. I followed her.

"This was your father's room," she said.

No shit, Sherlock. It looked like my room at home—if I was into peace signs, and Jim Morrison, and rock concerts in muddy fields.

"Make yourself at home. The bathroom's across the hall. Dinner is served at eight."

When I nodded, she went out and closed the door behind her. I wondered what I was supposed to do in the meantime. I had almost an hour, so I decided to check out the room, then clean up.

Everything seemed to be the way it was when Billy left home—his posters and books and records, even his clothes in the closet and shoes under the bed. Except there was no dust. Someone had to be cleaning it every once in a while.

Rosa was in the library, reading. She put the book down when I came in and looked at me like she was waiting for me to ask her something.

So I said, "You read all these books?"

"All of 'em."

"Wow!"

"I been workin' here a long time."

"They—Mrs. Wilding doesn't treat you very well. Why do you stay?"

She laughed. "The way humans is made, you can't take care of somethin' without comin' to love it or hate it.

"An' Mr. Wilding—when he was still hisself—treated me with respect."

"Did you know Billy?"

"Your daddy. He was the best of the lot. They didn't 'preciate that till he was gone." She shrugged and got up. "Mrs. Wilding had me set up with the good china for dinner. Wear your church clothes."

Dinner was worse than final exams. We were all dressed up—except Rosa, who was still in her nurse's uniform—and there was no one there but the Wildings and me.

There was enough silverware around each plate for two people—two forks and three spoons and two kinds of knife. I was starting to panic, when I caught Rosa's eye. "Start at the outside an' work in," she whispered. "Watch your grandmama."

Rosa didn't eat with us. She tied a small tablecloth around Grandpa's neck, like a giant bib, and fed him like a baby. Mrs. Wilding sort of ignored them. She asked me all sorts of questions: How was I doing in school? What sports did I play? Did I have a girlfriend?

I asked her pretty much the same questions about Billy.

"He used to date your mother. I didn't think they were serious until they ran away and got married. Just as well, I guess."

We were almost finished with dessert when she asked, "What made you decide to trace your roots now?"

So I told her about Dad getting killed. And that pretty much ended the small talk for the rest of the meal.

John

Saturday took me to Chicago on business. I got there early. A cold breeze off the lake and a brief early rain combined to turn the sun-warmed streets misty and mysterious. I parked in one of the overpriced city garages and walked to my appointment. Afterward I moved the Jeep to the Grant Park garage so I could visit the Art Institute.

As a boy, I'd read how Daedalus built the maze to imprison the Minotaur. The first time I'd entered the Chicago treasure trove, I felt Daedalus had had a hand in its design. But on subsequent visits, I came to realize it was more a labyrinth—convoluted, but not confusing—than a maze. Like classic labyrinths, despite its twists and turns, it formed a single path to a center—representing God in certain schemes, enlightenment, or art, or some similar grail.

Each of the famous artists represented a break with previous conventions, were rebels with a cause, Picasso being the most obvious. I could relate to rebels.

I'd visited often enough to have developed favorites: Whistler's *Nocturne*, Wood's *American Gothic*, Georgia

O'Keefe's *The Black Place.* I wished I had someone I could share them with.

Eventually, I found myself standing in front of *The Portrait of Dorian Gray*, marveling—again—at how perfectly Albright captured the idea behind the story. If an artist harnesses aspects of his own soul in his work, what did the picture say about Albright? And what did my preferences say about *my* soul?

Edward Hopper's *Nighthawks* held me the longest, embodying the loneliness I'd felt of late, the isolation.

I left wondering if Rhiann Fahey appreciated art, if I dared ask her to join me here some afternoon.

Jimmy

I spent Saturday with the Wildings—with my grandmother, really—Grandpa Wilding wasn't ever all there even when he was in the room.

He was white-haired and thin as a skeleton. He was always in a suit, with a tie, but I bet he hadn't dressed himself. He mostly stood like a lost sheep, or sat and stared straight ahead. When he talked, he didn't make much sense; sometimes he seemed to be talking to ghosts. Later I found out that he had to have someone take care of him all the time, and usually that was Rosa.

Mrs. Wilding mostly talked about Billy. She called him "your dad." I figured I didn't need to tell her Mickey Fahey was my dad.

She had a big black Lincoln, old, but cherry. When I

admired it, she handed me the key. "You may drive."

Yikes!

We went around to the post office, a stationery store, and the Stop & Save, where she didn't buy anything but she did give the manager a check. She introduced me to people by saying, "This is my grandson, James Wilding."

I felt like telling her my name is Jimmy, but I didn't. Something told me nobody *ever* told her she was wrong. And anyway, I figured I could use James Wilding as an alias if I ever had to take it on the lam.

Sunday morning, I woke early and lay in bed listening for sounds that somebody else was up. The house was quiet as a graveyard. Pretty soon, I got bored. I got up and dressed for church even though—judging by last Sunday—the Wildings wouldn't be going to church until almost noon.

I could smell the coffee before I even got into the kitchen. Rosa must be working already.

I was really surprised to find Steve at the stove with an apron over his Sunday suit. "Where's Rosa?"

"Sunday's her day off."

"Who—?"

"If I'm free, I come over and give your grandmother a hand. Otherwise your aunt Rachel or Liz comes over.

"Who's Liz?"

"Bobby's oldest kid."

"What's she like?"

"Oh, mean as a mongoose and ugly as sin."

Just then, the oatmeal started boiling—all over the

stove. Steve said, "Shit!" and forgot whatever else he was gonna say about my cousin Liz.

He turned out to be a pretty good cook. We ate in the kitchen—griddle cakes and eggs and bacon and juice and coffee. When we were done, Steve handed me the keys to Mrs. Wilding's car. "After you wash the dishes, you can bring the car around front."

"Who usually drives?"

"Me."

"I thought you lost your license."

"I got a special hardship license for Sundays."

"Yeah, right."

He held up his right hand. "Swear to God." Then he picked up the tray he'd fixed for the Wildings and took it upstairs.

After the service, Mrs. Wilding showed me Billy's grave and said, "I'll leave you to visit. Your grandfather can't be alone."

I wondered how long I was supposed to stay there, with a dead guy I'd never met. I didn't point out that *my grandfather* was with Steve.

The headstone was *big*:

WILLIAM O. WILDING 1952–1970
LOVING SON
BELOVED BROTHER

It didn't say anything about husband or father. I'd have to ask Ma about that.

I was thinking I should go back and find the Wildings

when I heard a stagey voice call out, "Jimmy. Jimmy Fahey." Like a kid trying to sound like a grown-up.

I whirled around, half thinking it was a ghost. But whose? Would Billy Wilding know I went by Fahey?

Nah.

So odds were it wasn't a ghost but a practical joker. Same problem. Who in Greenville would know me?

Then it said, "Jimmy," again, and I located the source—a big hole at the bottom of a hollow tree. The tree was alive, a maple with lots of big old leaves, so you couldn't see the upper branches.

I walked over to it and looked up.

And saw Beth! Very much alive, dressed for church. She was sitting on a branch next to the hole at the top of the hollow trunk, swinging her bare feet.

"You are one weird chick," I told her, wondering if I'd get to see up her skirt.

In the deep shade, I couldn't see her face, but her answer was clear enough. "Thanks a lot!"

"And if you're not careful, that branch is gonna let go, and you'll end up down here with the rest of the stiffs."

She wrapped her skirt tight around her legs and stuck out her tongue.

"I was at the library Friday night," I added. "You never showed."

"My dad wouldn't let me go out."

"You were grounded?"

"My life is one long grounded."

"What are you doing here anyway?"

"Taking a break from my family. How 'bout you?"

"Ditto." It seemed like a weird thing for me to say,

standing next to Billy's grave, but it didn't feel like he was family. And I didn't feel like explaining Billy to Beth. Instead I said, "You come here every Sunday?"

She suddenly dropped down to hang upside down from the tree branch. Her skirt flew over her head, and her arms dangled. She had the kind of outfit under—now over—her skirt that the girls wear in gym class. And she had really nice legs.

She reached up and grabbed the branch with her hands, then swung down, landing on her feet.

"Gymnastics?" I asked.

"Yes." She dusted off her hands. "And no. I don't come here every Sunday, just when I'm not working." She seemed kind of excited, like someone with good news or a neat secret.

It made me feel like I was in on something cool. "Where do you work?" I asked.

"At the Greenville Animal Hospital."

"What do you do?"

"Help the doctor. Feed the animals and clean their cages. Let the dogs out for exercise and brush them. And like that. You work?"

"Yeah. At a car repair place."

She nodded as if that figured. And I s'pose it did. I was a guy.

She started walking toward the church. I followed. She stopped in front of a really big statue of an angel marking one of the graves.

Except for its wings and long, old-timey skirt, the angel looked like a housewife. She was sitting on an overturned bucket with a broom across her lap and a garbage can lid leaning against her leg. On her lap, there was a real purse and a real pair of dressy shoes.

Beth picked them up and patted the statue's knee.

"Someone you know?" I asked.

"Just some lady who died before I was born. But her angel doesn't mind watching my stuff."

I stared at the statue. "It doesn't look that old."

"The statue's not. It's only been here five or six years. Her family must've won the lottery or finally saved up enough for a really good marker." She patted the angel's knee again. "I mean, this isn't some off-the-shelf stone from the local undertaker. It was carved by a famous artist."

"You think?" I stepped closer. I didn't really care about the statue but it seemed like a good excuse to get near Beth. She smelled great.

"I looked him up at the library."

She suddenly looked around as if she'd heard someone coming. I did the same—no one but us in the whole graveyard. She relaxed a little, but said, "I've got to get back before they miss me."

"I'll walk you."

"No. Thanks, but my dad'd kill me. And anyway, I've got to rinse my feet off before I put my shoes back on. Pick me up at work Friday, at six."

She gave me a wicked smile. Then she disappeared through a little door in the back wall of the church.

Rhiann

Jimmy and I were having dinner together Monday night. He'd filled me in on his weekend—sort of—and school. I'd gone on too long about my office. As he helped himself to the last scrap of pot roast, he grinned and said, "Ma, you ever eat at the Eat Well diner?"

"I used to work there."

"No shit! Doing what?"

"Waitressing."

"You? A waitress?"

"What's so incredible about that?"

"I'd think you woulda decked some rude dude and got fired."

I laughed. "I was younger and less confident then. More forgiving. I met your dad at the diner."

"Steve didn't tell me that."

"He probably didn't know."

"He talks like he knows everything about you."

"Nobody knows everything about anyone."

"Dad did." He stopped suddenly, and shivered as if someone had stepped on his grave. Or as if he'd realized, again, that his father was gone forever. He backed away from the table and took his dishes to the sink. There was a loud silence as he rinsed his plate and put it in the dishwasher. Then he said, "I'm meeting Finn at the library."

I gave him an is-that-so look.

"Really. He's gonna explain the mysteries of geometry. I'm gonna show him how to change his girlfriend's oil."

"At the library?"

"At his house. After." He leaned over to kiss me on the cheek, reminding me again of how he was growing up.

"Be home by ten-thirty."

"Yes, ma'am." He shook his head as he opened the door. "A waitress, huh?"

I sat there, recalling the first time I met Mickey.

February 1971. It was snowing and I was supposed to be home. Ma had jury duty and couldn't watch Jimmy, so I'd called in sick.

"I don't care if you're dyin'," Henry told me. Get in here."

"I don't have anyone to watch my kid."

"So bring him with you. Doris fell and broke something. She's at the hospital getting it looked at. Sara didn't show an' she's not answerin' her phone. Mary's coughin' up a lung. So I'm here all by myself."

"Where's Mike?"

"In Florida by now."

"Shit!"

"Yeah. Get in here."

I'd warmed up the car while I folded Jimmy's playpen and stowed it in the trunk. Then I bundled Jimmy into the car seat.

At the Eat Well, I took Jimmy inside and shoved him at Henry so I could go back out for the playpen and diaper bag.

"Hey," Henry yelled, startling Jimmy awake. "What'm I supposed to do..."

I was out the door; I didn't hear the rest.

When I struggled back in with the baby gear, Henry was out of sight and Jimmy was screaming and kicking in the arms of a stranger who resembled a grizzly bear. He had a full beard and mustache, and unruly brown hair escaped from beneath his Elmer Fudd hat. He was six feet tall and looked as big as a linebacker in his winter coat and boots.

The man spotted me and was clearly relieved. "Let's trade," he said before I could comment on the situation.

I dropped the diaper bag and leaned the playpen against the nearest table. I couldn't get my infant away from him fast enough, and my thanks wasn't especially gracious. Jimmy stopped crying immediately. I started toward the back, where, presumably, Henry was hiding out.

"Ma'am," the stranger called out.

I stopped, turned, looked him in the eye for the first time.

He seemed confused, concerned. He pointed at the playpen. "Where'd you want that set up?"

For a moment, I was speechless, the moment it took me to realize what he was asking and why. I looked around, decided on a quiet corner out of the traffic pattern, and pointed. "Over there."

He mirrored my nod and started to cross the room.

"Wait," I said.

He waited.

All I could think to say was "Thank you." This time I meant it.

He responded with an amazing smile that I couldn't help returning before I charged out of the room to tackle Henry.

John

I was coming home from Overlook one afternoon, passing the Catholic cemetery, when I noticed a raccoon curled like a fur-covered basketball—an ax-knot of pain—on the left margin of the road. There're no ambulances for wildlife; no one picks up their tabs. Even the task of putting one out of its misery is problematic. You can't shoot it at five P.M. on a residential street, and without a firearm, raccoons are not easy to kill. I thought about turning the Jeep around and finishing what the bastard had started who'd hit it. But I knew that wouldn't work.

I'd tried, once, to finish off a squirrel left thrashing in agony on the road. I'd aimed my left front wheel at it. But even though I was dead-on when it came to flattening discarded cans, I couldn't manage to touch the squirrel. I ended up stopping to end its misery with my tire iron.

I wasn't going to try that with a raccoon—they were too much like dogs. I couldn't beat a dog to death. So this time, I kept going. I called the police when I got home. I couldn't think of anything else; I don't own a gun. I doubted that the cops'd do anything, but I felt marginally better for having called. I got a beer from the fridge and went to drink it on the front porch.

I'm not sure what perverse impulse made me park my butt where I could see—through a break in the cemetery trees—the stretch of road where the raccoon lay breathing its last. Whatever it was let me see the sad denouement.

A familiar sheriff's police car pulled onto the shoulder and Deputy Sinter got out. He looked around—presumably for witnesses—then pulled his service revolver and emptied it into a spot on the parkway below my field of vision.

Then he stood there, looking down at whatever he'd shot while he reloaded his gun.

Rhiann

"I'm sorry." John had caught me crying again.

It was overcast and humid all day, with rain a possibility. I was sitting on my porch steps, wallowing in melancholy, when he pulled up after work. Getting out of his Jeep, he paused to say hello. He stood next to his car as if not sure what else to do.

"Not your fault," I assured him.

He nodded and took his lunch box and a paper grocery bag from the vehicle. "You okay?"

I didn't answer immediately. I felt I would never be okay again but—

"Stupid question," he said. "Sorry."

I shook my head. "I need to think of something else."

"Not always possible, especially so soon."

I gave him a little smile and changed the subject. "How're you and Jimmy getting along?"

He put his lunch box on the Jeep's hood. "He's a great kid. Not afraid to work."

Music to a mother's ears.

John was still holding the paper bag. He shoved it at me. "Would you like a beer?"

I had to think about that. Not good. Time for some

normalcy. "Sure."

He took a six-pack of Leinenkugel bottles from the bag and opened one for me, opened another for himself. The bottles clouded with condensation. "Cheers."

I held my bottle up and smiled. "Thank you."

He didn't ask for what. We sat taking in the cold beer and the warm evening. A red-winged blackbird sang. Bees buzzed among the peonies.

I felt a twinge of déjà vu. I used to sit just so with Mickey after work. I felt tears brimming.

John said, "You were married a long time?" Was he psychic?

I wiped my eyes with my palm. "Fifteen years."

He nodded and took another sip. He didn't offer platitudes, just quiet company—the way Mickey had sometimes.

When our bottles were empty, he said, "Another?"

"No. Thanks."

He put the empties in the holder and put it back in the bag. He picked up his lunch box. His "good evening" sounded sad, I thought. He walked slowly to his house, like a much older man.

Another wave of déjà vu jolted me as I remembered…

"Who's the new guy?" Doris tried to wipe the sweat from her forehead, hit it with the cast on her wrist, and muttered, "Damn it!"

I looked towards where she was facing, at the new customer in the back booth. The man who'd set up Jimmy's playpen the day before. "I don't know his name, but he's nice."

Doris shook her head. "He's got the thousand-yard stare."

"What?"

"The look they come back with, from Vietnam. My dad used to call it 'combat fatigue.'"

"You think he's a Vietnam vet?"

She shrugged. "My uncle served in Korea. He had that look." Doris was twenty-five and felt she had to fill me in on things. *Her* kid was ten and sometimes her advice was helpful. Now she said, "Some of those guys are baby-killers."

"I'll wait on him."

"I'm not saying he's one."

"My husband's in Vietnam."

"And look where that's got you."

I picked up the coffeepot and stalked away.

The newcomer looked up as I got near.

"Hi," I said. "My name's Rhiann. What can I get you today?"

He looked past me, toward the empty end of the lunch counter. Or maybe at something farther away.

"Sir? Earth to—"

"Sorry. Coffee. Scrambled eggs and bacon. Biscuits and gravy."

I turned over the cup that was standard with the table setting, filled it, moved the cream and sugar closer. I repeated his order and added, "Coming right up."

"Thanks." His smile never got to his eyes.

• • •

He came in every morning after that, and sometimes for lunch or dinner. Eventually, he introduced himself—Mickey Fahey. After observing that a few other vets were served without a hassle, he admitted that he'd recently mustered out. Unlike his fellow vets, he didn't complain about the country's antiwar attitude or the hippies who hung around plotting their protests over endless cups of coffee. In fact, nothing seemed to get a rise out of him.

Except Jimmy. Sunday mornings, when my ma went to Mass and other times when she couldn't watch him, I'd bring him to work with me. He was a good kid, usually entertaining himself quietly in his playpen. Mickey Fahey seemed amused by him. When he thought no one was looking, he'd make faces at Jimmy, or play peek-a-boo.

Mickey wouldn't talk about himself—not even to say what he did for a living now that he was a civilian, but he was full of curiosity about my son. I was grateful for his interest.

"You don't have any kids yet?" I asked him.

He just shook his head.

One day he said, "It's none of my business, but where's his dad?"

I fingered my wedding ring. "MIA."

"God! I'm sorry."

"Not your fault."

He tried to make amends by leaving too large tips. And one day, when I was working by myself and Jimmy started screaming, by picking Jimmy up. Mickey sat him on the table in his booth and played with him until my ma showed up to claim him.

After things slowed down, I brought Mickey a piece of blueberry pie.

"I didn't order this."

"But you'll like it. And I owe you."

"No you don't."

I gave him my don't-mess-with-me look, and he laughed.

"You ought to do that more often," I told him.

His smile faded.

I said, "Let me know how you like the pie," and went back to work.

It was late September when Mickey first asked me out. Billy was still MIA, but no one had offered me any hope that I'd ever see him again. Jimmy was a blessing and a distraction, but I was burning out—every minute scheduled, work at home or at the diner.

My second wedding anniversary rolled around. I didn't consciously mark the date, but I was mourning Billy.

Mickey came in for dinner and said, "What's wrong, sunshine?"

I thought about it, remembered the date, and burst into tears. He put his arms around me and held me until my sobbing ceased. I'm sure he waved Henry and Doris away. He sat me down in the back booth—his usual place—and got me a glass of water and some paper napkins to blow my nose on. Then he left me to pull myself together while he bussed tables and refilled everyone's coffee. Henry didn't try to stop him, just said, "I ain't hirin' you."

After I stopped crying and blew my nose, while I was trying to hide the damage with powder and fresh eyeliner, Mickey came and sat across from me. He didn't speak for a while.

Eventually, he said, "When was the last time you went out for a drink or a movie?"

I shrugged. "Before Jimmy was born."

"Tell me about your husband."

I looked around. Henry was waiting on the last customer of the night, Doris cleaning the empty tables. I sniffed. "Maybe someday."

He put his hand over mine. "Not tonight, but sometime, you should do something fun." He smiled. "Just for you."

I smiled back and patted his cheek. "You're a nice man."

His smile faded. He got that faraway look on his face. "I'm trying."

I turned him down three times in the next three weeks. He came in every night for dinner, and once a week he'd ask me out for a drink.

"I'm a married woman," I told him the first time.

"So. I'm not asking you for a date, just a drink."

I shook my head. "Thanks, but no."

The next time, I said, "Not tonight."

The third time, I begged off on account of Jimmy.

"My mother'll watch him. She can't wait to be a grandma. It'll be good practice for her."

How could I refuse? Especially since Mickey made a point to invite us to his mom's for dinner a week ahead of time so Jimmy and "grandma" could get acquainted.

Our first nondate was a Friday night, at a little country-western bar that had good beer and live music. Mickey knew the musicians. Just before last call, they made him sing—his choice, anything he liked. We'd been listening to the music for hours, nursing Leinenkugels. The lead singer came over and shoved his mike in Mickey's hand and said, "Your turn."

Mickey tried to beg off, but the guy was adamant.

Finally, Mickey said, "Okay. But only if you can play my song."

"Anything. We can play anything."

"'You Are My Sunshine'?"

"No sweat."

Mickey sang it to *me*.

John

The summer settled into a rhythm. When school let out, Jimmy Fahey came to work full-time. I paid him for forty hours and he always put in at least that many, though he came to me in mid-June and asked for weekends off.

"To visit your girl?"

He blushed. "Yeah, but don't tell my ma."

"Well, if you can't be good, be careful."

He turned bright red and said, "I gotta get this battery out."

When Jimmy told me about his grandfather Wilding, it was with a combination of fear and fascination. "You don't seem surprised," he concluded.

I shrugged and quoted Shakespeare on the ages of man. "That's life."

He told me that the Wildings had a library bigger than the Overlook Public Library. "All those books," he said. "Mr. Wilding can't read 'em and Mrs. Wilding won't. Nobody reads 'em except Rosa."

"Rosa?"

"She's their maid. I think. They—Mrs. Wilding treats her like a slave, but it seems like she really runs the place."

"So you've mastered an important lesson on the nature of power."

I could see him thinking about that for a minute. Then he said, "What do I win?"

I held up the part I'd just extracted from the Ford we were repairing. "The chance to rebuild this carburetor."

"You and my dad would've really hit it off. I mean my real dad. Not Billy Wilding."

Praise indeed.

Jimmy

The Greenville Animal Hospital was just east of town, between the highway and the river. There were four parking spaces out front and a driveway that went behind the building. When I got there, a big guy in a lab coat was helping an old lady get her hairy white dog in her car. After she and the dog drove away, the man walked over to my Chevy and said, "Help you?" The name on his coat was Dr. Pulaski.

"I'm supposed to take Beth home."

"You her boyfriend?"

"I wish."

He nodded. "She'll be done shortly. You can drive around back and wait."

"Thanks."

I parked facing the building, with my car backed up to the river side of the rear lot. I sat on my back bumper to wait, and watched a dragonfly zoom over the water like a miniature helicopter. I lost track of time.

I almost landed on my butt when someone jumped up and down on the front bumper, making the car rock like a boat. I whirled around to see Beth hide a laugh behind her hand as she balanced on the front of my car.

God, she was beautiful! Her blond hair was pulled back in a ponytail, but little wisps had gotten loose and made a halo around her face. She was wearing jeans and a long-sleeved shirt made of some white stuff you could almost see through.

I slapped my hands over my chest and said, "You tryna give me a heart attack?"

She giggled. "Your heart's not that weak." She went to the passenger side and waited for me to open the door for her—like my ma always did when she was dressed for church.

So I did.

I got in, and before I started the car, I said, "What now?"

"We go somewhere, and you tell me all about yourself. And I tell you enough about me so you'll want to know me better."

"You want to get something to eat?"

She sighed. "Only if you're buying. I'm broke."

"'Course I'm buying. What do you want?"

She shrugged.

"Mickey D's?"

"What if—"

"If the goons are there, we'll go to DQ."

The goons weren't at McDonald's. So I bought us dinner. To go. And we drove to the library parking lot to eat it. The lot was empty since the library was closed. The weather wasn't real hot, but after we finished, we took off our shoes and hung our feet out the car windows and traded life stories. Sort of.

I told her about Ma and my dad. And my cousin Steve. Only I left out his last name. I didn't tell her about the Wildings, either. I figured everybody in Greenville knew Mrs. Wilding—or at least, knew about her. And I didn't want Beth to think I was crazy by birth.

She told me she had two brothers and overprotective parents—overprotective of her. They let her brothers do whatever they liked. She said she'd lived in Greenville all her life and was a junior in high school—now that she'd passed her finals.

I asked her about her job.

"I love Dr. Pulaski," she said. "He's a great boss."

"Like, I'll bet you had a lot of bosses to compare."

"Five. I'll tell you about them when I know you better."

That was promising.

"What's your boss like?" she asked.

"I like him. He never yells or swears, even if he slips with a wrench. When he has a cool repair problem, he makes everybody stop what they're doing and watch how to fix it. And lots of times, when you ask him a question, he answers by asking *you* questions until you come up with the answer on your own."

"Where do you live?" she said.

"Overlook—technically outside the city limits, on a bluff over the river. The town's on a patch of ground above the high-water line. They built it more than a hundred years ago, where there used to be a ford, which was replaced by a ferry, then a railroad bridge, then a bridge for cars. Now we got a modern four-lane highway bridge with a sign that says HISTORIC ROUTE 66."

"How'd you know all that?"

"Had to do a report on it in seventh grade. Mr. Ricci—my history teacher—wasn't happy just making us learn dates and names, we had to know the reasons for things."

"Like what?"

"Like luck plays a big part in life. Like World War Two happened because Hitler was a shitty painter."

"That's silly."

"No, really. If he'd been a decent painter, he never woulda gone into politics."

"You're kidding, right?"

"Cross my heart."

We hooked up with Stephanie and her boyfriend, Nate, at the drive-in. Steph parked her car next to mine and we went back and forth during the coming attractions, with the girls giggling about stuff and me and Nate checking each other out.

When the movie started, Beth and I got back in my Chevy and scrunched together in the front seat. Stephanie and Nate stayed where they were. By about halfway, though, I managed to get an arm around Beth without pissing her off. I looked over and saw Nate had passed first base and was closing on second.

"How long have Steph and Nate been going together?" I asked.

She looked annoyed, then confused, then said, "Since freshman year. Why?"

"I just wondered."

I guess I'm not a good liar, because Beth looked over at the other car, then bit her lip. It was too dark to see, but I'd bet she turned red.

"You want some popcorn?" I asked.

"No. Er—Yes." She glanced at the other car and said, "Maybe you should ask them."

"Thanks a bunch."

She giggled.

I made sure I accidentally tapped the horn taking my arm from around her shoulder. Out of the corner of my eye, I saw Stephanie and Nate straighten up and look around. It was too dark to tell, but I'd've bet they were both red, too.

I leaned over and opened the glove box, and palmed a couple of Trojans from my stash.

"What's that?" Beth asked.

"Guy stuff." I got out quickly, so I didn't have to show her, and tapped on the window of the other car. Nate was in the driver's seat. He rolled the window down. "What?"

I handed him the Trojans. "Get a room," I said, softly,

so Stephanie wouldn't hear.

"Fuck you."

"No, thanks." Louder, I said, "You guys want some popcorn?"

After the movie, the four of us went to the Dairy Queen to shoot the shit before Beth and Stephanie had to show up back at Steph's house.

It seemed like we barely had time to finish our ice cream and fries before Steph said, "We better go."

"Yeah," Beth said, "before your mother comes looking for us."

We were on our way out the door, when Beth's face got white as her shirt.

I said, "What's up?"

She just pointed to a familiar car pulling into the DQ lot. The Greenville goon mobile.

Nate said, "Oh, shit!"

"What do we do?" Stephanie asked.

"You and Beth get the hell outta here. I'll create a diversion. Get 'em outta here!" I told Nate.

"They'll kill you," Beth protested.

I waved at the full parking lot. "Not in front of all these witnesses. You gonna be at the church tomorrow?"

"No. I have to go to work."

"See you there."

"But—"

"Go!"

She left, with Steph and Nate pulling her along.

I went out the door on the other side of the lobby—right into the middle of the Greenville goons.

I had the element of surprise on my side, and years of studying the Fonz. I pulled out my comb and ran it through my hair. It got their attention; I was the only one who noticed Stephanie's car pull out of the lot.

I didn't get too far into my impersonation before the head goon threw the first punch. I stepped back, but not before the other two moved in.

"If it isn't Fraidy Fahey," the first goon said. "Where you gonna run to this time, chicken?"

"He who fights and runs away lives to fight another day." I took a quick step back.

I wasn't quick enough. One of them got me in a full nelson. He was big enough to be a linebacker, and his buddy started whaling on my rib cage.

I tried to kick number two in the shins, which bought me a second to think.

Dad taught me how to get out of a full nelson. I raised my arms as high as I could and pushed the backs of my hands against my forehead. Then squatted. Goon number two was strong, but not strong enough to hold a hundred seventy pounds out in front of him.

I slipped out of his hold, rolling and kicking at goon number one. I connected with his ankle before his buddies got their game on and started using me for punting practice.

I curled up, trying to protect my head and kidneys and the family jewels.

Dad always said, "Getting the crap beat out of you isn't brave or manly. It's stupid. Don't be afraid to call for backup when you're outnumbered."

It was plain I needed help. I was about to start screaming like a girl, when the DQ manager came running out with his Louisville slugger.

I slipped onto a bar stool just before closing, figuring any cops who might bust me would be outside somewhere waiting to snag the drivers staggering out with their travelers. Steve was working on autopilot. He threw a coaster down in front of me and said "What'll it be?" before he realized I was his underage cousin. When he actually looked at me, he said, "Jesus!"

"You shoulda seen the other guy."

He glanced around at his customers, then dug into his ice chest and filled a bar rag with ice. As he handed it to me, he said, "You mess with somebody's girlfriend?"

"Somebody messed with mine."

"Two weeks ago you didn't have a girlfriend. Fast work."

I didn't have a comeback.

He went around and collected the empties, emptied the ashtrays, and called last call. Then he settled everybody's tab and escorted the stragglers to the door.

Meanwhile, I made myself useful by putting the chairs up on the tables.

"You looking to crash at my place?" Steve asked.

"Can I?"

"What if I said no?"

"I guess I'd sleep in my car."

He didn't say anything more. He filled the mop bucket with Spic and Span and handed me the mop. While I did the floor, he wiped the bar and washed the glasses and took out the trash. Then I helped him restock before he locked up.

In the car he asked, "You gonna make this a regular gig?"

"If it's okay with you."

"What re you gonna tell your ma?"

"That I got a Saturday job in Greenville."

"And a girlfriend?"

I shrugged. "Sooner or later."

The next morning, I drove Steve to the Eat Well diner for breakfast. Carol gave my shiner and bruises a look, but didn't say anything, so when we were finished, I left her a big tip. Then Steve and I went to the Stop & Save where we filled a cart with groceries.

"I could get used to this," he told me when we pulled back into his drive.

"How do you usually get your stuff home?"

"Five or six trips on my bike."

"What do you do in the winter?"

"Hitchhike. And eat out a lot."

"You ever gonna get your license back?"

He shrugged. "You plannin' on coming every weekend?"

"Probably."

"Then we better stop at the hardware and get you a key."

Sunday morning, I dropped Steve off at the Wildings' and headed to the animal hospital. It was closed, but Dr. Pulaski was there to check his patients, and Beth to feed them and clean their cages. I knocked on the back door.

When Beth opened it, she turned white. "What happened?"

I'd forgotten about stopping the goons' boots with my face. "You should see the door," I said.

"What?" She looked like she thought I was crazy.

"I ran into a door. Pretty lame, huhn?"

"I knew we shouldn't have left you."

"I'll live. Are you ready to go for a drive?"

"No, I've got sixteen dogs and three cats to take care of."

"I'll help you."

By the time we finished, it was too late to go anywhere if I wanted to get Beth home before her folks got suspicious. Dr. Pulaski seemed fine with me driving her—it meant he didn't have to. He locked up and took off.

Beth and I sat on the riverbank for a while and dangled our feet in the water because neither of us wanted to say goodbye. I told her about being rescued by the DQ guy; she told me she'd lectured Stephanie about going too far with Nate. I didn't mention the Trojans. We skipped stones across the river. Little bluegills swam up to our feet, then darted away. I kissed her cheek.

"Your dad ever gonna let you date?" I asked.

"Maybe when I'm twenty-one."

"In five years?"

She punched my arm playfully. "How old are you, Methuselah?"

"Seventeen."

"What're we going to do?"

"How 'bout you leave your window unlocked, and I'll sneak in after dark?"

"My father would catch you and beat you to death."

We sat there with our feet in the water, letting the fish nibble our toes.

Then Beth said, "I know! I'll tell my mother I've got a regular Friday-night babysitting job. You can pick me up at work and drop me off at home after dark."

"Sounds like a plan to me."

Rhiann

"Did you stay with your grandparents?" I asked Jimmy when he got home Sunday night. I was putting the clean dishes away.

Jimmy plopped down on a stool at the island counter. He crossed his arms and rested his elbows on the countertop. "Nah," he said. "With Steve."

"He has a drinking problem."

"He doesn't have any booze in his house."

"You checked?"

"Well, I noticed."

"Are you planning to go back this weekend?"

"I kinda thought I would. Something wrong with that?"

"The house is so empty."

I knew I sounded lonely because he said, "I could fix you up with someone."

"Like who?"

"How 'bout my boss?"

"Don't be silly." Too much, I realized. "What makes you think he even likes me?"

"I've seen him look at you the way Finn and me look at Meg Ryan."

I blushed and changed the subject. "How *is* Steve?"

Before he called to say he'd met Jimmy in Greenville, I hadn't thought of my cousin Steve in years. He hadn't come to Mickey's funeral. Maybe he didn't know. But I'd called my parents and they'd called his. My aunt and uncle sent flowers and a Mass card with their condolences. Not a word from Steve.

Steve and Billy had been best friends long before I moved to Greenville. Then they and I and Smoke had been inseparable through junior high and high school. Till Billy joined the army and Smoke disappeared.

Steve stayed home with me. But since I'd made it clear my heart was taken, he'd just been a good friend. Good enough to stand up for us when Billy and I tied the knot. Good enough to hang around and help with Jimmy until Mickey came on the scene.

Then Steve drifted away—into drink and bad company. When I tried to stand by him, he'd told me to "fuck off."

"What's the matter with you?" I asked.

"I always wondered if you kissed me would I turn into a prince." He was a little drunk. Happy drunk. "I knew I didn't have a chance with Smoke and Billy around, but they're gone..."

"You're too much like a brother." I kissed him on the cheek. "And you're already a prince."

He made his eyes go wide and spread his fingers out. He peered down at one hand, then the other. Then looked at his feet. Then he gave a little smile and shook his head. "Still a frog."

I laughed.

"You better marry the Mick. It's plain he worships you. And he'll be a good example for the kid."

"Are you giving me your blessing?"

"Yeah. But don't ask me to stand up for you at the wedding."

"Will you come?"

"Sure. I'll sit in back and cry."

Strange that Steve would meet up with Jimmy after all these years.

Thursday afternoon, Jimmy was peeling potatoes for me while I cut up the beef for stew.

"Hey, Ma," he said. "When you were growing up with Billy, did you know Rosa?"

"Sure. But I called her 'Mrs. Jefferson.'"

"Mrs. Wilding told me to call her 'Rosa.'"

"Didn't she also tell you to call her 'Grandmother'?"

He grinned and swept the peels into the covered bucket we used for compost.

I said, "Could you empty that for me?"

"What do I get?"

"The privilege of taking out the trash."

"Cute, Ma." He grabbed the trash bag by the door and took it and the compost out. When he returned, he said, "Ma, remember that creepy deputy sheriff that always sits in the front row at church?"

"Rory Sinter."

"Yeah, him. Why's he watching our house?"

"I don't know, but next time I see him, I'll ask."

John

With Jimmy gone on weekends and business booming, I saw less of Rhiann Fahey. Probably just as well. I felt like a teenager around her, putting my foot in my mouth and tripping over my tongue. As a countermeasure, I'd clam up, and there'd be awkward silences.

Occasionally, during the week, she'd invite me to join her and Jimmy for barbecue in the backyard. I went out and bought a Weber so I could reciprocate.

Fourth of July, the three of us sat on my porch roof and watched the fireworks blossom over the river below the cemetery.

Rhiann and I *did* go to an amateur theater production in Alva. *Our Town.* And out to dinner afterward. She sounded sincere when she said she'd had a good time, but on the porch, she didn't drag out her "good night" into an invitation.

Just before she closed the door, she said, "I'm sorry, John. I'm just not ready to move on."

Rhiann

The sheriff's office was on my way home from work but—in spite of Rory's reminders—I'd passed it every day without remembering to collect Mickey's gun. After Jimmy told me about Rory hanging around, I stopped in to get it.

Sheriff Linden had been a real friend of Mickey's, so I was surprised when he didn't take my complaint about Rory seriously. "He's just lookin' out for his friend's widow, is all."

"I don't need to be *looked out for*."

"Rory told me about Devlin—did time for killin' a man."

"He deserves a second chance."

"To kill somebody?"

I scowled.

"Look, Rhiann, Mickey told me you were a Christian woman. An' I know forgiveness is a Christian virtue. But blind trust isn't."

I just shook my head and said, "Can I have Mickey's gun?"

"You got a firearms card?"

I took my wallet from my purse and dug out my FOID card.

The sheriff glanced at it, then got Mickey's gun from a drawer in his desk, broke it open, and handed it to me. Then he pushed a box of shells across the desk. "I don't guess I have to tell you to be careful."

Jimmy

By the middle of July, I had the summer thing down pat. Monday through Friday, I worked for John. Friday afternoon, I drove to Greenville and helped Beth finish up at the animal hospital—Dr. Pulaski broke down and hired me. Then we'd get something to eat and go for a drive or go bowling or to the drive-in. Sometimes we'd double-date with Stephanie and Nate. Others we'd just go somewhere and talk. Saturdays, we'd work at the animal hospital and go out after work. On Sunday, if she worked, I did, too. If it was Beth's week to go to church with her family, I'd help Steve close up Hannigan's Saturday night and head home after dropping him off. Or I'd stay over and go home early in the morning.

I was ready to kiss Beth the first time we met, and every day I saw her after. But I had a hunch she wasn't ready. And we had Nate and Stephanie's example to warn us about how fast you could get in over your head if you weren't careful. They were really into each other, going through half a dozen condoms a week—which Nate got from *my* glove compartment. At least they were being careful, but I was the one supplying the protection. Me and John.

One Saturday night in mid-July, Beth and I went to see this movie—*Summer School*—about a bunch of losers who end up making it because of a coach that gets drafted to be their summer school teacher. We went to the early show 'cause Beth had to be home. We were just coming out of the theater when the Greenville goons pulled up in front, heading west—the same way we had to go to get back to my car.

Beth saw them first. "Now what do we do?"

At that point, one of the goons spotted us and shouted. The driver braked hard. Too hard.

An old guy following them in his Cadillac didn't brake fast enough. There was a screech and the crunch of metal crumpling as the Caddy folded up the goon mobile's rear end.

I took Beth's arm and headed her east. "Plan A."

"What's that?"

"Hang on to your hat and run like hell!"

Before I took Beth home, we stopped at the Eat Well diner. I was amazed she'd never been there before. "You *do* live in this town?"

"Yeah. My dad's kind of a snob. He said this place is a dump."

"Has he ever eaten here?"

"Probably not."

"I'll bet the goons never come in here, either. But if you like we could go someplace else."

"Oh, no. This is perfect."

It was Beth's church-with-the-family weekend, so after I dropped her off, I stopped at Hannigan's to say good-bye to Steve.

There was this big guy nursing a beer at the bar. He had an empty shot glass and a pile of dollar bills in front of him. He chugged the rest of his beer and slammed the glass down. "Bartender, set me up again."

"Sorry, pal," Steve said. "We already had last call."

The guy looked around. Other guys were still shooting pool. A couple that was dancing stopped to put another quarter in the jukebox. The night-shift cop who was packing away a cheeseburger lifted his coffee mug, and Steve took the pot over to refill it.

When Steve got back behind the bar, he put out a couple drink trays. I took one and started collecting empties.

"Fuck you, asshole," the boilermaker drunk told Steve. "I want another setup."

Steve said, "Sorry. No can do." He grabbed a bar rag and started away from the guy, polishing the bar as he went. And he started whistling—"Bad Moon Rising."

The drunk got up and followed him along the customers' side. When Steve ran out of bar, the guy grabbed his shirt and tried to pull him across the bar.

"Hey!" Steve yelled.

Everybody in the room stared.

The drunk let go.

Steve held up his hands. "You've had enough, sir." He was talking loud enough for everybody to hear.

The drunk swayed a little and said, "I'll decide when I've had enough."

The cop sighed and got up and put on his hat.

The drunk threw himself on the bar and rolled over it to trap Steve against the kitchen door. As he drew back for a punch, Steve grabbed a drink tray and held it over his stomach—just before the drunk's fist connected.

The guy howled and shook his hand.

Steve held the tray up like a shield.

When the drunk drew back to hit him again, the night-shift cop grabbed the guy's wrist and snapped handcuffs around it.

It seemed like everybody had to deal with bullies, even Ma. When I turned onto my street the next morning, I noticed that creep Sinter watching the house again. He wasn't even pretending he was doing radar—he had his dome light on. He saw me and sneered. At least, I thought he did.

And I wondered what it would take to get him to leave my ma alone.

Rhiann

Jimmy was pretty well housebroken for a teenaged boy. He emptied and took out the trash and took his turn cutting the grass without being asked—most of the time. He usually did his own laundry.

But as the summer went on, he seemed to be more and more pressed for time. I suspected that he'd met a girl, though he never mentioned one. Things started piling up in his room.

So one evening, when I needed to make up a full load of laundry, I gathered up everything on his bedroom floor. There were some heavy items in the pockets of his Levi's. I went through them and found a small wrench, a spark plug, and an Eisenhower dollar. I had to stop and sit down when

I found the Swiss army knife because a sudden sense of loss echoed through me like a timid "miserére" in an empty church. I knew the knife. The sight of it reminded me that Mickey was gone, although—to my knowledge—Mickey had never seen the knife. I hadn't seen it myself since the day Billy was declared KIA.

They came on a Sunday. They were waiting on the street, in their government-issue car, when we pulled into the drive after Mass. Two soldiers in dress greens. A young one—still in his teens—and an older man with the same thousand-yard stare Mickey had brought home from Vietnam.

Dad noticed them first. He didn't say anything, but his look clued my mother, and she said, "Oh, no!"

I was taking Jimmy out of the car seat. At my mother's words, I got a queasy feeling. The September sunlight lost its warmth. Jimmy picked up on my distress and started fussing as we watched the soldiers get out of their car.

My parents took positions like sentries on either side of us.

The sergeant stopped in front of me and took off his hat. "Mrs. Wilding?"

I nodded. I don't remember the rest of his words. I remember my mother taking Jimmy, my dad putting his hands on my arms, holding me up when the sergeant held the knife up, along with Billy's dog tags.

I must have confirmed that the knife was really Billy's. He put it and the dog tags in the box he was carrying. Billy's stuff. He offered the box to me.

I couldn't take it. My father steered me to the porch steps and sat me down before talking to the soldiers and taking the box off their hands. I told him to throw it away, but he'd said, "Maybe Jimmy will want it someday."

Seems he was right.

Now, I put the knife with the other pocket junk on Jimmy's dresser, then gathered up the clothes and fled the room.

John

In school, my best friend was a poor rich kid whose father was a self-made millionaire. I was white trash. I think that's part of what drew my friend to me. I was definitely someone of whom his father would disapprove.

We had other things in common. We both hated his brother for one. "You must've been switched at birth," my friend told me. "He's as mean as your old man."

My friend and I both loved the same girl, but we never competed for her. I think she favored me, but didn't want to hurt his feelings. So we hung around with her together; and neither of us made a move.

Then he joined the army. I got drunk and killed a man. I went to jail and did five years.

You can read a lot of books in five years. I cultivated the prison librarian, and he adopted me. He gave me Gideon's

Bible and the Koran. Shakespeare. Mark Twain. Joseph Campbell and Joseph Heller. Tolstoy. Just to name a few. I learned a trade, discovered I had a talent, earned a GED.

I wasn't without remorse but I'd served my time.

By then my friend was dead. The girl had married someone else.

My life went on without women and with few friends.

Then I moved to Overlook. I bought my first house. And after Rhiann Fahey took me to the church supper, I started going to services. I'd sit in back and watch her pray, or sometimes grieve. And watch Rory Sinter ogling her.

It didn't take a Ph.D. in psychology to read her body language. Sinter irritated her, sometimes made her mad. She wasn't intimidated. And he didn't seem to pose a threat, so I stayed out of it. I waited. Watched. Was ready to intervene if intervention was required.

It wasn't just at church. Sinter did radar on our street, though fewer than five cars passed by on any given day. I never saw him make a stop. I made a point to travel slowly.

One day he stopped me anyway. A hot afternoon in late July. Sinter was sweating behind his mirror shades. I kept my hands on the wheel until he said, "Get out of the car."

I got out.

He shoved me up against the Jeep and frisked me. "License and registration?"

"License is in my wallet; registration's on the visor."

He pointed to my back pocket. "Take it out."

I handed him the license.

He studied it carefully. Looking for signs it was a fake? Or something out of order?

"Registration?" He kept his hand on the butt of his gun

as I reached inside the car. "Slow an' easy."

Did he think I was reaching for my .30-06?

He compared the two documents as if they might disagree in some fundamental way, then asked, "You got anything in your ve-hic-le I might need to know about?"

"No."

"No, sir!"

"A dozen apples and a six-pack of Coke." I didn't mention the box of condoms. He'd surely take *that* the wrong way.

"Real funny. Mind if I have a look?"

"As a matter of fact, I do."

"Why's that?"

"If you had probable cause to search my car you wouldn't need to ask."

"You must be one of those jailhouse lawyers."

I didn't answer.

He handed back my documents and said, "You can go."

I moved slowly—no need to give him an excuse. For what? I didn't want to push him to find out.

He stood sweating behind his state trooper glasses with his hands on his hips as I put my license away and got in the Jeep. His effort to seem cool was undermined by the circles of sweat beneath his armpits.

Then he slapped the roof and said, "Drive nice." He stepped back as I put the Jeep in gear.

"Next time, I'll have a warrant."

Jimmy confided that he'd been stopped, as well.

I asked him to elaborate.

"The guy's a creep," he said, and told me what had happened. He'd gotten the same general BS I had, but he'd been speeding. Not speeding carefully enough.

"To be fair, he could have given you a ticket."

"I guess I'd rather have the ticket. I don't want to owe the jerk."

I didn't tell him how often I'd seen the deputy watching for a chance to nail him. Or me. Or maybe Rhiann. Or that I'd watched Rhiann myself. Watched her come and go. And hang her laundry out. Watched her garden, wash her car, read her paper on the front porch. She never seemed to notice.

I understood Sinter's obsession, if not his stalking.

I yearned for the woman with every fiber in me and felt her nearness strangely comforting. For the first time in my life, I was content.

Jimmy

"What're you going to be when you grow up?" Beth asked me one afternoon.

It was the beginning of August—hot—and we were sitting on the bank of the swimming hole Steve told me he swam in when he was a kid. It was out in some farmer's property but it wasn't posted so it seemed okay to be there. We had our feet in the water. It was almost dark. Fish were jumping and the mosquitoes were starting to bite.

"We should bring fishing poles," I said.

"You didn't answer my question. And what would we do with fish?"

"Eat 'em."

"Raw?"

I looked to see if she was kidding; she couldn't keep from laughing.

"Naw. We could fry 'em on my exhaust manifold."

"Really?"

I grinned. "Gotcha!"

"You still haven't answered my question."

"What was the question?"

She gave me a stern look, so I stopped kidding around. "A cop."

"Like your dad?"

"Yeah." I slapped a mosquito on my neck.

"You don't have to be a cop just because your dad was one."

"I know."

"Why?"

"Why what?"

"Why do you want to be a cop?"

I shrugged and gave her the answer Dad used to give me. "It's honest work. The pay's good. And someone has to do it."

"You want to be a hero, don't you?"

I looked closely at her. She wasn't kidding.

"Doesn't everybody?"

She thought about that, then said, "Most people, I guess."

"What do you want to be?"

She squished a mosquito on her arm. "A veterinarian."

"You'll be good at it."

"If I can get into vet school."

"You will."

"You're not the least bit prejudiced."

I couldn't help it—I leaned over and kissed her. She didn't pull away.

When I did—finally—I said, "I'm sorry."

She looked hurt. "Wasn't it good?"

"Oh, yeah."

"Then why are you sorry?"

I just shook my head and kissed her again. And she kissed me back. I had to quit before I got too carried away.

"What?" she demanded.

"I love you."

She leaned her head against my shoulder. "I wish summer would never end."

"Might as well enjoy it while we got it." I pulled off my shirt and dropped my jeans.

Beth stared at my boxers and pretended to be shocked.

"C'mon," I said. "Last one in is a—"

She gave me that I-dare-you-to-say-it look.

"Sissy." I grinned and dove in.

After that, it was hard not to think about going all the way. I wanted to. And she would've, but she was only sixteen.

"When's your birthday?" I asked her one night. We'd been parked on a deserted street near her house, making out. We were both pretty excited; I had a hard-on.

"September."

"September what?"

"Why? You gonna buy me a present?"

"Maybe."

"September twenty-first."

More than a month away.

Just before Labor Day, Beth and Steph suckered me into driving them to the megamall down on the interstate "to shop for school clothes." It was between Greenville and Overlook—no big deal for me, but I hadda put up a little fight. "Only if I can watch you try them on."

"We'll model them for you," Beth offered.

"Deal."

The highway went through the top of a big hill, about five miles from Overlook. When you started down the slope, you could see the whole valley, down to the river, and my street and the two cemeteries and the layout of the town. From the top of the slope, everything looked tiny, like the miniature trees and houses on a train set. I wished I coulda blown off the mall and kept going to show it to Beth. I bet she would've loved the view.

We were two miles from the mall when I noticed that we'd picked up a tail—the goonmobile. "They got that heap fixed pretty fast."

"What heap," Beth asked. "Who?"

"Three guesses and the first two don't count."

She looked back and spotted our tail. "What are we gonna do?"

"Plan B."

Steph said, "What's Plan B?"

"Improvise."

I speeded up a bit. The goons did, too.

I got into the left lane, floored it, and got about a half mile ahead, just before a curve that I knew was a big speed trap. As soon as I got around the curve, I moved over and slipped in between two big semis. The goons came around the curve accelerating, doing at least twenty over. They missed us completely. And they missed Deputy Sheriff Sinter doing radar up ahead. Until he put his flashers on.

I slowed down even more to let him into traffic in front of us. So we got a great view of the pull-over.

"God, Jimmy," Beth said. "They're gonna slaughter you if they ever get their hands on you."

"They gotta catch me first."

Rhiann

In August, the rights-of-way are blue with cornflowers and white with Queen Anne's lacy parasols. I was on my way home one afternoon, taking in the beauty, when I noticed Rory doing radar—just after I passed him. I was fifteen miles over the limit.

Rory had to have noticed me but hope springs eternal. I took my foot off the gas but didn't brake. Either he wasn't paying attention or he'd decided to cut me some slack. He didn't pull out after me. I wondered why, then put him out of mind.

I always speed, ever since I was fourteen and the three guys I grew up with taught me to drive—cars they *borrowed* when we needed wheels. We always returned them, sometimes with more gas than when we left. We got really good at avoiding the police. In retrospect, we were insane.

Smoke was the best driver. He was normally fearless. And he was more patient—at least with me—than Steve or Billy were.

Billy was the most careful, Steve the most persistent.

By the summer Smoke was sixteen, he'd saved enough to buy a '61 Ford that had bald tires, a bad clutch, and missed on half its cylinders. Steve, Billy, and I spent a lot of time on weekends and evenings helping him fix it up. We worked overtime at our jobs to put new tires and other parts on it. But then we had our own wheels. With our own chauffeur. Smoke owed us, but he would've driven us anyway because he loved driving. And he would *never* let anyone else drive his baby.

He'd picked me up one day, on our way to join Steve and Billy. But he took the long way around—down a farm road with long stretches of straightaway between the driveways. He put the pedal to the floor, and the speedometer needle went all the way to the right.

I sank back in the copilot's seat and squeezed the armrest until my knuckles turned white.

Smoke eased off the gas. "You can't be scared," he told me. "You gotta accelerate into the curves and downshift when you brake. If you know what you're doing, you'll never lose control."

Then he pulled over and let me take the wheel.

John

I was a child of the sixties, weaned on rock and roll. I learned to appreciate country music in prison, when I was forced to listen. Before that, I associated it with my abusive father. At Stateville, I bunked with a guy you didn't mess with. He left me alone, but he insisted we listen to "real music"—country-western. He had a hundred pounds on me, so I didn't argue. I noticed that when he turned the volume up, it drowned out much of the hideous noise from the tiers; I couldn't miss the lyrics. For the first time in my life I was forced to see that country music always tells a story. I came to love the storytelling aspect.

The summer and fall of '87, my life became a country-western song.

I wanted Rhiann Fahey so badly it hurt. It hurt to see her every day. It hurt whenever I didn't.

Jimmy went back to school in September. I missed having him underfoot.

Deputy Sheriff Sinter—always lurking in our neighborhood—reminded me of ballads about badass outlaws. As far as I could tell, he was a rogue cop.

And there was no one to report him to.

Jimmy

After three months of working at a real job and seeing my girl on weekends, school sucked. I still worked after school, but being around John made me realize that school would be so much better if there were teachers like him. I lived for weekends.

Before I left for Greenville one Friday in September, I left Ma a note: "I'll be late Sun. Nite. Don't wait up." Sunday was the day before Beth's birthday. She was spending it with her family, who were giving her a party. After the party, when they were all in bed, Beth and I were gonna celebrate together.

There was a new moon. We hadn't had a hard frost yet, so the crickets were singing. I parked on the street around the corner from her house and waited. And fell asleep.

Beth woke me when she opened the passenger door to get in. I got a quick look at her dress before she closed the door and the dome light went off. "You look great," I told her.

"Thanks. Let's get out of here before the neighbors see us and call the police."

As I started the Chevy, she said, "I brought something."

"What?"

"Let's go somewhere private and I'll show you."

I used my parking lights to navigate the road out to the swimming hole. It wasn't real dark—there were about a billion stars out. And a million crickets doing their thing. Beth leaned over and rested her head against my shoulder. When I'd parked facing the water, I turned off the lights. I left the motor idling because it was starting to get cold. I said, "Let's get in the back."

"We need some light."

"Got that covered. C'mon."

Beth dug her bag out from under the seat and got out.

I'd borrowed an old quilt from Ma's linen closet and thrown it over the back seat. On the floor I'd left a candle lantern and kitchen matches. I lit the candle and set the lantern on the dashboard. Wedged against the windshield, it wouldn't tip no matter how much we shook the car. And the glass sides kept the candle from blowing out.

We got in. Beth took a bottle out of her bag.

"What's that?"

"Champagne. From my party." She took two clear plastic cups out of the bag. "You ever had champagne?"

"A sip, maybe. At a wedding."

She handed me the bottle. "You can open it."

I unwound the little wire holding the top on.

"You'd better hold it out the window." She got the two glasses ready.

I twisted the plastic cork back and forth until it shot off the bottle, sending up a fountain of foam. "Wow!"

Beth laughed. "That's what it does inside your head. I think. Anyway, every time my mom has some she and my dad go upstairs and lock their door."

I grinned and pulled the bottle inside and filled the glasses. I wedged the bottle on the floor between the front seat and the door. "Wait." I leaned over the front seat to get

Beth's birthday present out of the glove compartment. "Put those glasses on the back ledge."

When she did, I handed her the little velvet box I'd gotten at the jewelers.

Her eyes lit up like a kid's on Christmas morning. She opened it very slowly. The sapphire pendant inside glittered in the candlelight.

"Oh, Jimmy! It's perfect." She took it out of the box by its gold chain, and held it up. "Put it on me."

In the bad light, it took a lot of fumbling to get the little fastener closed, but it was worth it to see how happy it made her. She stood up and leaned over the front seat to see it on herself in the rearview mirror. She turned around and threw herself on me in a big hug.

"We need a toast." I reached for the glasses and handed one to her. "Happy birthday!"

We drank to that. The wine made my nose itch and my head spin. "Awesome."

Beth grinned.

"You sure you want to go through with this?" I asked her.

She nodded. She finished her champagne and put the glass back on the ledge.

"What do we do?"

"I'm supposed to kiss you until you're ready."

"How will I know I'm ready?"

"You just will." She didn't look convinced. I wondered what kind of sex education classes they had at her school. "You've seen dogs do it, right?"

"No-oo. We don't let them—"

"Forget I said that. Didn't your mom ever—?"

"My *mom* said I should wait until I'm married and my

husband'll tell me what to do."

"Jesus!"

"Don't swear."

"Sorry. Let's start over. Why don't I just kiss you and see what happens?"

We both leaned forward. And bumped heads. It was funny and we laughed. Only it wasn't funny because she'd never even let me feel her very far up before. And now we were trying so hard to make our first time special and romantic like in the movies but it was getting more like a stupid sitcom.

I started to unbutton her dress. I could feel that *I* was getting ready.

She said, "This isn't your first time."

"No, really. It is."

"How do you know all this stuff?"

"My ma's got this book—*Everything You Always Wanted to Know About Sex*—she keeps right out in the open, in the living room bookshelf. I studied it."

Beth grinned and pulled off my T-shirt.

"Hang on a second," I told her. "I almost forgot something." I leaned over the front seat again. There was just one condom left in the glove box. Dammit, Nate! I grabbed it and dropped down next to Beth.

We got her dress off. I'd seen enough movies to remember to hang it carefully over the back of the front seat. Underneath, she had on this sexy white bra and panties.

Beth noticed the effect they were having and pointed at the bulge in my pants. "What's this?"

I sucked in my breath.

She said, "Can I see?"

I unbuckled my belt. She unsnapped my fly and pulled the zipper down. "What's in here?"

"Your new pet."

She giggled. "Can it do any tricks?"

I hauled it out and said, "Let's see."

She stared at it. She giggled again.

I felt hot. I leaned into the front seat to turn off the engine. While I had my back to her, Beth pulled down my pants. When I turned back around, I shook them off and rested my knees on the back seat on either side of her, and leaned back against the front seat.

She kept staring at my dick like she'd never seen one before. Maybe she hadn't. It was distracting.

"Can I touch it?" she asked.

"Sure!"

When she did, it started to come to attention.

Her eyes widened and she leaned away. "It's so big!"

I grinned but I thought she looked worried. Maybe it was *too* big.

Hoping to set her at ease, I asked, "How 'bout a little more champagne?" I got the bottle and refilled our glasses.

She practically chugged hers. I took it easier; I could feel it going to my head. My dad had warned me that booze can ruin your love life.

Besides, I was enjoying the view.

I put our glasses back on the ledge, and lowered her onto the back seat, slipping a finger under her bra strap. "Isn't this uncomfortable?"

"A royal pain." She licked her lips.

I kissed them. Then I fumbled her bra off and kissed her beautiful boobs. By the time I got her panties off, I was ready.

And she was willing. When I licked my finger and slipped it inside, she moaned, "Yes!"

I was ready to run for home.

Then I remembered. "Protection!"

"What?" She half sat up.

"Where's that condom?"

"I don't know. Who cares?"

I felt around over the seat and finally located it. I almost dropped it getting it out of the wrapper. Our candle sputtered out. I'd gotten it half on by feel when Beth froze under me.

"What was that?"

"Was what?" I could feel the fun fading.

"I heard a noise."

We both held perfectly still while we listened. The crickets had stopped. Cold seeped into the car. I felt the condom slip off, heard it hit the floor.

"What was *that*?" Beth whispered.

I whispered back, "My last condom down the drain."

Across the water, an owl hooted. Out on the highway, a truck backfired. Somebody laid on their horn for half a mile.

Beth took my head in her hands, and I could feel her shaking underneath me—whether from fear or cold I couldn't tell. We waited until the crickets started up again and we couldn't take the cold anymore. We didn't hear anything threatening.

Finally I whispered, "Maybe we should go to Plan B."

"Maybe you should just shut up and hold me."

Which I did. The last thing I remember was pulling the old quilt around us and feeling her silky skin warm against mine.

• • •

There was just the slightest bit of pink in the eastern sky when I woke up. The car was freezing, but it was toasty under the old quilt. And Beth was warm and soft. I started getting hard.

I leaned away from her and touched her cheek. "Wake up, little Suzy."

She opened her eyes slowly. "Where—What time is it?"

"It's sunup. Happy birthday." I kissed her on the shoulder. Her skin burned my lips.

She smiled and stretched. "Good morning."

Her face glowed in the dawn light, and I couldn't help it, I kissed her. She kissed me back.

We kissed and touched until nature took its course.

I had a sudden recollection and pulled away.

She grabbed my hair with both hands. *"Don't stop!"*

"I'm out of condoms!"

"I don't care!"

She grabbed my dick and guided it inside, then wrapped her legs around me for dear life.

And *oh, my God*!

It was the most beautiful sunrise of my life.

Rhiann

Monday morning, Jimmy wasn't home. I didn't notice right away. I got up and started breakfast. When he didn't come downstairs at the usual time, I yelled up to him. "Jimmy, you're going to be late for school."

There was no answer, so I went to wake him. The room was empty. His bed hadn't been slept in.

The numb disbelief I'd first felt when they told me Mickey was dead started to fill my mind like silt clogging a vacuum filter.

Why hadn't he called?

How could God let this happen to me twice?

Then my common sense kicked in. Jimmy was a teenager. Boys his age stayed out all night. If he'd been experimenting with booze again, I could only hope he'd had the sense to sleep it off. Mickey and I always insisted we'd drive to hell to get him—no questions asked—if he got drunk or stranded with someone who was planning to drive drunk. And if he'd had a breakdown, it was fifty—mostly rural—miles between Overlook and Greenville. If he'd had a breakdown, I'd hear from him sooner or later.

I decided to go to work. If something bad had happened, the police would let me know.

Jimmy

"Drop me off here." Beth was smiling and there was something different about her. She seemed less giggly, more definite.

It was still early, but we were pushing our luck. I stopped next to her neighbor's hedge so my car was hidden from her house.

"I hate to let you go," I said.

"Let me out. If anyone sees me come in, I'll say I went out to get the paper." She pointed to the rolled-up newspaper lying at the end of her driveway.

"What if they see you come from over here?"

"I'll say it was such a beautiful morning I went for a walk."

"I want you. I-want-you-I-want-you-I-want-you."

She laughed. "You'll see me Friday."

"No shit!"

"Kiss me good-bye. Quick. I gotta get ready for school."

I had less than two hours to get home and to school, and my brakes were starting to feel a little soft. Need to check the fluid. One more damn thing to do today. I didn't let it bother me, though. After this morning, nothing was gonna bother me.

I turned up the radio and pushed the buttons until a moldy oldie station started blasting out the Moody Blues—"The Story in Your Eyes." One of my folks' favorites, that I'd grown up listening to. I turned up the volume and put the pedal to the metal.

I was still booking when I came over the hill above Overlook. I had about twenty minutes to get to the house, grab my books, and make it to school before the bell. Halfway down the hill, I figured I'd better take it a little slower and I started to brake.

Nothing happened.

I was speeding up. Getting close to the T-intersection at the bottom of the slope. I pumped the brake. The pedal went to the floor. Still nothing happened.

Except the car kept going faster.

I downshifted. Looked for the safest way to turn. Traffic was coming from both directions on the cross street.

I pumped the brake again—from habit. I shifted down one last time and leaned on the horn. Just before I blew past the stop sign, there was a tiny break in traffic from the left.

I jerked the wheel to the right and floored it into the turn. Too fast. I would have tail-ended the car I tore in behind if I hadn't cut onto the shoulder. Horns blared.

I felt a wheel catch in a rut. Something snapped in the front suspension. The steering wheel jerked out of my hands. The car seemed to take off over the ditch. A *big* ditch. I was suddenly airborne.

Last thing I remember was somebody screaming, "Oh, shit!"

Me.

Rhiann

The police *did* let me know. I'd been at work an hour when Sheriff Linden came into the office, hat in hand, and strode up to my desk.

"Mrs. Fahey, your son's been in an accident. He's pretty bad. I'll drive you to the hospital."

In the car he said, "According to the witnesses, your son ran a stop sign and took the corner too fast—where the road

Ts at the bottom of that hill near your house. He went off on the shoulder and hit the tail end of the guard rail. Went airborne and rolled over. If he wasn't wearin' his seat belt he'd be dead."

I stared straight ahead and tried to relax the stranglehold I had on my purse strap. I didn't say anything until the sheriff pulled up at the emergency entrance and said, "Anybody I could notify for you?"

"My cousin Steve Reilly. In Greenville." I released my seat belt and reached for the door handle. "Thanks, Sheriff."

He took his seat belt off, too. "I'll walk you in."

The hospital staff were used to dealing with hysterical mothers. One of the nurses put an arm around me and steered me to the admitting counter, where another woman in nurse's scrubs explained that Jimmy was being prepped for surgery. He had a concussion, and a compound fracture that had to be repaired. I could help by signing an authorization to let them go ahead. He needed blood, too. If I could donate, it might give me something to do during the wait.

I signed a pile of papers, promised to pay if we didn't have insurance. I would have signed my soul away to get on with it and see my son.

The first nurse came back and led me into the heart of the building, where Jimmy lay on a gurney, white and still as a corpse.

Inside, I felt as dead as he looked.

They let me touch him. And kiss him. Then they wheeled him away.

John

When Jimmy didn't show up for work Monday afternoon, I didn't think too much about it. It was the first time he'd blown me off, but he was at the age where an occasional lapse was to be expected. By four-thirty, I was uneasy—the kid was too reliable. I called the house and got no answer. I finally called Rhiann at work.

Her boss picked up. "Farmer Shipping."

"Mr. Farmer, is Rhiann Fahey there?"

"Who's calling?"

"Her son's employer. Jimmy didn't show up for work today."

"That's because he's in the hospital. He crashed his car."

"How bad?"

"Bad."

I went to the hospital on the outside chance that I could give blood or something. They were just a little too eager when they found out that my blood type was A negative, pushed me to the head of the line and rushed my contribution off to the lab as soon as they pulled the needle from my arm. They gave me juice and cookies and told me to take it easy for a while. For some reason, they seemed to think I was family. When I asked about Jimmy, they sent me up to the ICU waiting room.

Rhiann was there, deep in conversation with a man about her own age, so she didn't see me. Not wanting to interrupt, I took a seat near the elevator.

Within a few minutes, a doctor arrived. After a short conference with Rhiann and her friend, the doctor and Rhiann went into the ICU, leaving her companion staring after them.

They came out five minutes later.

"He's stable," the doctor told us, "but he'll be out of it for hours." He looked pointedly at Rhiann. "Meanwhile, you should get some rest."

"I can't."

The doctor shrugged and left.

Rhiann noticed me and made introductions. "Steve, this is my neighbor, John Devlin.

"John, my cousin Steve."

"You the guy Jimmy works for?" Steve asked.

"Yes."

Rhiann was still looking at me. "You heard the doctor?"

I nodded. "From what Frank Farmer said, it sounded pretty serious. I came to see if I could help."

"That's good of you." She shook her head. "There's nothing we can do except wait. And pray."

She started to go back into the ICU, to Jimmy, then stopped. "Could you take Steve to my house? And bring him back in the morning?"

I felt the green-eyed monster creeping up. I stifled it and said, "Surely."

Steve started to protest, but Rhiann said, "Please, Steve. You can call my parents for me. I can't deal with it. And you can spell me tomorrow."

He shrugged. "Can I get you coffee or something before we go?"

She shook her head and smiled. I'd have given ten years of my life to have her smile at me like that. "I'll be all right," she told him. To me, she just said, "Thanks, John."

As we passed the blood bank, the phlebotomist hurried out.

"Mr. Devlin." She handed me a fist-sized red paper badge, heart-shaped and self-adhesive. "I forgot to give you this."

It said, BE NICE TO ME. I GAVE BLOOD TODAY.

"Thanks," I said, hoping Steve hadn't noticed. "That won't be necessary."

She kept holding it out, so I grabbed it and stuffed it in my pocket.

Steve didn't comment. We rode in silence for several miles before he asked, "Do you believe in God, Devlin?"

I shrugged. He waited.

I finally said, "It's hard to sometimes."

"Yeah. I *know* that kid. He's stayed with me all summer. Never got a clue he would drink, much less drink and drive. And he was a good driver. *Is*." Steve shook his head. "Rhiann doesn't deserve this." There was a long pause before he added, "If there *is* a God, he's a nasty bastard."

I dropped Steve at the hospital the next morning and waited until he was inside before I parked. The business office wasn't open for an hour, so I used the time to call my shop manager and get him started on the day. Then I went to the cafeteria to find out what I could about the hospital and the doctors who worked there.

Judging by the scuttlebutt, the hospital was a place its staff would be comfortable being treated. The surgeons thought they were gods, but maybe were. The ICU head nurse was Patton reincarnated for the war on death. The recovery-floor nurses were Mother Theresa's kin. I relaxed a little.

When the office opened, I arranged for Jimmy to get a private room—for which his mother would be charged the semi-private rate. And I made sure word of the arrangement would never get out.

They'd moved Jimmy into the surgical recovery unit by the time I got back that afternoon. The elderly woman at the front desk asked if I was family and gave me directions when I told her yes.

Jimmy was still unconscious, Rhiann and Steve still holding watch. They didn't seem to think I was out of line joining them.

Rhiann turned the TV on, turned it off, walked down the hall to make a call on the pay phone. Steve paged through all the magazines from the waiting area by the nurse's station. Then he came back in Jimmy's room and stared out the window. I offered to get takeout; no one was interested. Staff came and checked Jimmy's vitals. They reported there was no change and left. The boy slept. We waited.

Jimmy

The first thing I remember is hurting, 'specially my leg. I didn't want to open my eyes because they hurt, too. And even through my eyelids, the light seemed really bright.

I couldn't remember where I was. Or where I was s'posed to be. Or what day it was.

I couldn't remember my name.

That was *really* scary.

So I made myself open up and look around.

Ma was there.

I think I said, "Mom?"

I can't remember what she said, but I knew everything would be all right because Ma would take care of things.

I tried to ask her what she said. Or something. I don't remember. Everything was too much.

So I closed my eyes again.

And I guess I went back to sleep.

John

Jimmy opened his eyes around three in the afternoon. His first word was "Mom?"

"I'm here, Jimmy."

"What happened?"

"You were in an accident."

Jimmy said, "Oh," though he didn't seem to understand. He drifted back to sleep.

• • •

Around seven Deputy Sheriff Sinter dropped in. Steve was in the can. Under the circumstances, I hung back. I didn't want to start anything.

Sinter didn't notice me. He made a point to hug Rhiann. It was obvious she wasn't comfortable with that, but she didn't make a fuss.

"Rhiann," he said, "let me take you home. You're too tired to drive. You can take a shower and catch forty winks. Jimmy's in good hands. He'll be okay."

"No."

I stepped forward and said, "She has a ride."

Sinter froze. "What're you doing here?"

Rhiann stepped close to me and slipped her hand beneath my arm. "John came to drive me home."

Sinter seemed to think that over, then told her curtly, "Let me know if you need anything."

"Thanks. I will."

There was nothing else for him to do but leave.

Steve came out of the can and picked up on something wrong. He looked from her to me and back, waiting to be clued in. He finally asked, "What's up?"

"You just missed Trooper Sinter," Rhiann said.

"That creep you told me about?"

"Yeah."

He looked at me. "Good thing you were here." He looked at Rhiann. "You should get some rest. I'll stay with Jimmy."

"I couldn't."

"You can't do anything more for him tonight. The doctor said he's stable."

I waited, not willing to weigh in on the debate, though I, too, thought she needed sleep.

"Honestly, Rhiann," he continued, "you'll be more use to him when he wakes up if you're rested. Go home and get a shower. If there's any change I'll call you. Or you could come back here to sleep. But it'll do you good to get out of here for a while."

"I don't know."

"Devlin'll drive you—won't you?"

"Of course." I looked at her. "I'll bring you right back if you like."

"I'm so tired, I can't think." She rested her chin on her palm, supporting her elbow with the other hand.

Steve shook his head. "I rest my case. Take her home, Devlin."

I touched her shoulder. "How 'bout it?"

She nodded, and I put a hand under her arm to steer her out.

In the car, she spotted the crumpled paper heart I'd tossed on the seat and started sobbing.

I said, "I'm sorry—What?"

"That someone we've known for years can be such a jerk." She picked up the heart and turned it round and round. "And a virtual stranger so kind. Steve told me you gave blood!"

"Just a half hour of my time. I'll replace the blood in a couple weeks."

She dropped the heart back on the seat and got a Kleenex from her purse.

"Let's get you home," I added. "It'll be easier when you've had some sleep."

"Jimmy could die! How does that get easier?"

"He's in God's hands."

"Will you pray for him?"

"If it'll help you."

She sniffed and wiped her eyes. "You don't sound like a believer."

"I stopped praying when my mother died."

"I cursed God when He took Mickey. Do you s'pose that's why Jimmy—?"

"God wouldn't be vindictive."

In spite of what Steve said.

She started sobbing again.

I leaned over the gap between the bucket seats and pulled her against me. I held her until she drifted off, then eased her against the passenger door and put the seat belt around her. She slept until I'd parked the Jeep in her drive. She followed my instructions like a robot as I led her to her door and saw her safely in.

Rhiann

When I woke up, I couldn't remember, right away, how I'd gotten home. Then—John! He'd come to the hospital to check on Jimmy and rescued me from Rory.

Jimmy! I grabbed the phone. The nurse on duty told me Jimmy was fine—having breakfast as we spoke.

I dressed quickly. Levi's and Reeboks, a T-shirt and my crumpled linen jacket. Comfortable clothes. Comfortable shoes. I went downstairs to microwave some coffee but didn't have to. There was a tap on the back door as soon as I came into the kitchen.

I opened the door to John, holding two steaming mugs of coffee.

"I saw your lights go on," he said. "I thought you might need some caffeine."

I stood aside to let him enter. "You must be my guardian angel."

"Just a fellow addict." He put the mugs on the island, sliding one toward me. "I didn't know what you like in it."

I got out milk and sugar, which he declined. I added milk to my mug, returned the bottle to the fridge. Holding the door open I asked, "Can I fix you something? Ham and eggs? Or oatmeal?"

"Thanks, but I ate an hour ago. But *you* have something."

I sighed and stared in but couldn't recall what I was looking for. Breakfast. Nothing looked anywhere near appealing. Reason told me to make a choice. I grabbed a couple of individually wrapped sticks of string cheese. "These'll do."

He didn't comment on my choice. He said, "I'll take you back whenever you're ready."

"Will it be a problem if you're late for work?"

He shook his head. "One of the perks of being boss."

I slipped the cheese into my jacket pocket and picked up the coffee mug. "I'm ready."

He opened the door for me. I felt my pocket as I walked out—keys and wallet were there. The door locks automatically when you pull it shut—which he did.

He'd backed his Jeep into my drive so the passenger side faced the kitchen door. Now he stepped around me to open the car door. He closed it when I was in.

He drove fast, but carefully, not taking chances, not speeding enough to draw the law.

"You drive like Mickey," I told him.

"Is that good?"

"He was a great driver, very careful."

He accepted the compliment with a nod.

"Would you—" I said. "Could you teach Jimmy to drive like that? When he's better."

"I'd be happy to."

We went on in silence. I was too strung out and stressed to make conversation; he apparently didn't feel the need to talk.

I recalled that when I was very young, Steve and Billy and Smoke and I would go on hikes or hang out at the swimming hole, not speaking for hours. None of us ever had a problem with it.

When John stopped in front of the hospital, he handed me a business card with just his name and phone number. "Call me if you need anything," he said.

"Thank you. Thank you for everything."

"You'd probably do the same for me."

I watched him drive away—he didn't look back—but I had his number in my hand.

John

I was surprised when Frank Farmer stopped by the shop a few days after Jimmy's accident. I knew he was sweet on

Rhiann and saw me as a dangerous rival—closer to her age, and a threat because of my record.

I've found the best way to deal with hostile people is to pretend that we've never met and have no preconceptions about one another. So I said, "What can I do for you Mr. Farmer?"

"I wonder if you'd do a favor?"

I raised my eyebrows and waited.

"Not for me. For Rhiann Fahey."

"Name it."

He gave me a look that said, "It figures." I waited.

"The sheriff called me 'cause he knows she's still tied up at the hospital. They're done with Jimmy's car and pretty much want it outta there. You got a tow truck and you'd know where to take it till Rhiann's ready to deal with it."

"Certainly. I could bring it here." I pointed to a back corner of the shop. "We'll throw a tarp over it and leave it until Jimmy recovers."

He nodded. "I'll call the sheriff and tell 'em to expect you." He seemed to want to say something else, but he didn't.

I watched him get in his car and drive away, then went to get the truck.

When I got to the sheriff's impound, the deputy at the counter told me I'd have to wait.

"How long?"

"Don't know. Some insurance adjustor's comin' to look at it. Can't take it till he's done."

"Where is he?"

The deputy shrugged. "Called a half hour ago. Said he was on his way. Didn't say where from."

I thanked my stars that I had a competent crew back at the garage and asked the deputy if he'd like me to bring him anything from Dunkin' Donuts.

"Coffee'd be nice."

I nodded.

By the time I returned with two coffees and a dozen doughnuts, the insurance adjustor had arrived. He was middle-aged and overweight. His suit was rumpled, his tie stained. He climbed out of his Buick dragging an old leather briefcase bulging with papers.

I handed the deputy his coffee and dropped sugar packets and creamer on the counter next to the doughnut box.

The adjustor's lack of preparation confirmed the bad first impression he'd made—no flashlight or camera. He waddled over to the deputy and said, "You got a light?"

From his expression, the deputy's assessment of the guy was similar to mine. He got up and threw a switch on the wall behind him, turning on the overheads.

I followed as the insurance adjustor pulled a police report from his briefcase and dragged himself over to the remains of Jimmy's car.

The front end was caved in where it'd hit the guard rail. A tie rod was broken, and the right front wheel stuck out at a sickening angle.

I went and got the big Maglite and creeper from my truck.

The adjustor stood in front of the car and made notes on his clipboard. When he finally looked up from his report, he turned to the deputy. "Says here there was no skid marks leading up to the crash site. Kid didn't even try to brake. You know if they tested him for booze?"

"Don't know nothin' about nothin'," the deputy said. "Not my department."

There was a stain on the inside of the left front wheel that looked to me like brake fluid. When I pointed it out to the insurance guy he said, "Even if it is brake fluid, so what? Brake lines break during accidents."

On the opposite side from the point of contact?

"Mind if I take a closer look?"

"Knock yourself out. I'm done."

I dropped onto my creeper and slid under the wreck.

The impact had pushed the front end back into the motor, bending the frame and mangling just about everything forward of the front axle. But I could still see the brake drums, and the tool marks where someone had loosened the brake line.

I scooted out from under the car and called the insurance guy over. "Look at this," I said. "Someone sabotaged the brakes."

He shook his head. "Nah. You seen as many wrecks as I have, you could tell the difference between a bad crash and sabotage."

The deputy came out from behind his counter to look. He shrugged. "Don't see nothin'. 'Vestigatin' officer didn't neither."

I counted to ten.

The insurance guy shoved his clipboard into his briefcase and walked out.

The deputy shrugged and went back to his coffee and doughnuts.

I said, "Do you have a phone that I could use?"

He turned his phone around and pushed it across the counter.

I called the state police. They transferred me twice before connecting me to "a detective or accident investigator."

"Crowley."

"This is John Devlin, a friend of the Fahey family."

"Yeah. And?"

"Mickey Fahey's family. The officer killed last March?"

"What's up, Mr. Devlin?"

"Mickey's son, Jimmy, was recently injured in a serious accident. I have reason to believe his brakes were tampered with. It happened in county jurisdiction, but they don't seem to be interested in looking into the matter."

"You a detective or insurance investigator?"

"No. I'm a mechanic."

"So you'd recognize when brakes've been messed with."

"I would."

"Well, Mr. Devlin, I'm not in a position to come—Where did you say this car is located?"

"In the county impound garage."

"I'm sorry, but I can't get over there today. Maybe tomorrow?"

"They want it out of here today. I noticed the brake problem when I came to tow it away."

"Chance you could tow it over here?"

"Give me the address."

It had been years since I thought about the pileup that sent me to prison and the other guy to the morgue. It was a crash, not an accident. We were drag racing, and we'd both been drinking. Drinking and bragging in a little podunk roadhouse. It was late and raining, but we agreed to settle the question of who had the best nerves and better car out on the street.

Half a dozen equally inebriated barflies staggered out after us to witness the event. Fortunately for me, the bartender wasn't a race fan. He called the local law before we even got our engines started—he saved my life.

When my partner in criminal stupidity rolled his car into mine, he was killed instantly. He wasn't wearing a seat belt.

I was. Still, I would've bled to death if the sheriff hadn't arrived immediately after the crash and stanched the flow. Somewhere between the scene and the hospital, the paramedics poured enough fluids into me to bring my BAC down to 0.09. So the sheriff didn't charge me with DUI, just reckless homicide.

Crowley tore himself away from whatever he was doing long enough to come out into the state police garage and show me where to drop Jimmy's car. I waited for him to look it over. He stopped his cursory examination to ask me a question:

"If this does turn out to be something, do you really want some smart-ass defense lawyer asking you under oath if you hung around and tried to influence the investigator?"

"Point taken."

• • •

Three hours later I was back at work when Davey called out, "John, phone."

I picked up. "John Devlin."

Crowley's voice answered: "I checked up on you, Mr. Devlin. You're something of an expert on car crashes." He waited.

I didn't answer.

"But," he went on, "you kept your nose clean the last fifteen years."

It hadn't been fifteen years since I got out of prison—he must have talked to someone at Stateville.

"And you've got a good rep as a mechanic. So I looked real carefully at young Fahey's car. And I agree with you. The brakes were messed with. The fun part's gonna be provin' it. And findin' who'd want to kill a seventeen-year-old kid."

Rhiann

A few days after they moved Jimmy out of the ICU, Steve and I were in the hall outside his room, waiting for the orderly to bring him back from X-ray. Sheriff Linden got out of the elevator and approached me.

"Got to ask your son a few questions," he told me, "about the crash."

I told him where he could find Jimmy—lying on a gurney in the hall, waiting his turn at the machine. The sheriff started away, then stopped and held out an unmarked evidence envelope. "Might as well give this to you."

I took it. "What?"

"Your son's effects. Don't need 'em for evidence. He didn't have any alcohol in his blood, so he's not bein' charged with anything. Best if you take 'em home for safekeeping." He tipped his hat and stalked off toward the X-ray department.

I looked in the envelope, found Jimmy's wallet, some change, and the Swiss army knife. I took it out and stared at it.

"How did Jimmy get Smoke's old knife?" Steve asked, taking the knife.

"Smoke gave it to Billy the day he ran away to join the army."

"You saw him that day?" Steve sounded hurt, understandably. We were the Three Musketeers and D'Artagnan, and we three had gone on an adventure without him. He gave me back the knife and turned to the window to look out.

I didn't remind him he'd been grounded that week—for something Smoke talked him into.

"Billy needed a ride to the bus station in Overlook because he knew his father would find out and stop him if he left from Greenville."

Steve turned around and leaned against the windowsill, crossing his arms. "So he asked Smoke for a ride?"

"Yeah."

"But Smoke hated the army. And the war—even before anyone ever heard of Vietnam. Why *would* he?"

"He would've done anything for Billy."

Steve nodded.

"I sneaked out," I said. "And Smoke picked me up. Then we hooked up with Billy and drove to Denny's to wait for the bus. Just before it came, Smoke pulled out his knife and handed it to Billy. 'You need an army knife in the army, man,' he said. 'I'm never gonna join so you take it.'"

Steve said, "Jesus."

"Yeah."

"I'd've thought Smoke'd never part with that knife. Not after..." He turned back to the window and stared out.

I hadn't thought about Smoke in years...

He'd never talked about his parents or invited any of us to his house. Steve told me that was because his father was a mean, crazy drunk, and running into Tommy Johnson was like meeting Max Caddy, or the Wolfman under a full moon. I didn't believe it until the afternoon I met Smoke and Tommy coming out of the Pick'n Save. Smoke just nodded at me as if I were someone he knew slightly. Tommy ignored me. I was hurt but curious, so I watched them take their stuff out to their truck. One of the bags tore just as Tommy lifted it from the cart, sending cans flying in between the cars. Tommy began swearing like a soldier. At Smoke. Smoke got real quiet, started picking up the cans, fitting them into the untorn bags.

I knew him well enough by then to realize that the madder he was, the quieter he got. Obviously, something more was going on than a few spilled groceries.

Tommy didn't help clean up the mess he'd made, just stowed the rest of the bags in the truck bed and gave the cart a shove. It slammed into a parked Cadillac. Tommy didn't seem to notice. He got in the cab and yelled for Smoke to get in.

Smoke grabbed the last two cans and scrambled into the

cab before Tommy laid rubber pulling away.

Smoke cut school for the next two weeks. When he finally showed up, he had the ghost of a shiner around his left eye. Steve asked him what happened.

Smoke just grinned like he was letting us in on a secret. "I was trying to make it pop out—like a frog's—an' I guess I went too far."

That was all we ever got out of him, though Billy swore that Tommy hit him.

The year we were in seventh grade, Steve and I went to Florida with our families over Christmas. Billy's folks always took him somewhere cool—Acapulco or Italy—wherever. So we were all gone until just before school started, and none of us saw Smoke until after classes the first day.

He almost blew his cool-guy image, he was so glad to see us, but he waited almost an hour to show us what he got for Christmas—a Swiss army knife. Billy'd gotten a .22 from his father, but Smoke's knife was cooler—he'd carved a little frog on the handle. And—he was quick to point out—he could bring it to school.

He'd only had it a week when we were ambushed by four high school bullies, who demanded our lunch money and anything else we might have that they could use. Steve and Billy and I were ready to give it up without a fight, but Smoke stepped between us and them and told them to go to hell.

They forgot the rest of us and instantly zeroed in on Smoke, spreading out to surround him. We just stared.

One of the thugs jumped Smoke from behind and tried to get a hand in his pocket. Smoke threw an elbow in his ribs; the thug screamed and folded up. Two of them grabbed Smoke and the third punched him twice in the stomach. Smoke doubled over, then threw himself sideways into the one on his right, kicking the guy to his left as he fell to the ground. The thug with the bruised ribs grabbed Smoke's head; the first guy Smoke had knocked over grabbed Smoke's right wrist with one hand and and tried to empty his pocket. He got hold of the Swiss army knife.

Smoke went crazy. He head-butted the guy holding his head, and twisted around, breaking the second guy's grip. Smoke grabbed his knife, then spun around in a circle on his back, kicking the ankles of the two guys still standing, and the head of the thug whose ribs he'd hammered.

Before he could get up, though, the jerks regrouped. Staying just out of range, they took turns kicking Smoke, bloodying his nose.

Billy and Steve and I were stunned. We were used to threats from older kids, but not outright brutality. We had no idea what to do.

The blood made me crazy. I didn't think; I just knew they would kill Smoke if someone didn't help him. I jumped on the back of the nearest bully screaming, "Stop!" digging my nails into his face and neck. My scream must've woken Steve and Billy, because suddenly they were yelling and punching the high schoolers, too.

Rage evened the odds. When the bullies found themselves on the receiving end, they made like the cowards they were and ran. We actually chased them half a block before coming to our senses.

We stopped as abruptly as we'd started and, remembering Smoke, turned back. He was sitting with his elbows on his knees, head down, bleeding all over.

"Smoke! You all right?"

He wiped his bloody nose on his sleeve, then held up his knife and grinned. "At least they didn't get this."

Jimmy

The nurse told me I had a visitor, and before I could ask who, the state trooper came in. He was dressed in a suit, but I could tell he was a cop. For the first time, I was glad to have amnesia.

"You Jimmy Fahey?" he asked, even though I bet he already knew the answer.

"Who wants to know?"

He handed me a business card that said "Sergeant Dan Crowley, Illinois State Police."

"This about the accident?" I asked.

He nodded and sat down on the visitor's chair. "Can you tell me what happened?"

"I don't remember."

"What do you remember?"

"It's kinda foggy—I left home on Friday to go to Greenville. Then I woke up here."

"Who would know what you did over the weekend?"

I squirmed a bit. They'd told me the accident happened Monday morning. "Maybe Beth," I admitted. Or not.

He rested his elbows on his knees and leaned forward.

"Who's Beth?"

"My girlfriend."

"What's her last name?"

"I don't remember."

"Cute, kid."

"No. Really. I have amnesia. Ask the nurse."

"You remember what you were doing in Greenville?"

"I have a job there Saturdays and every other Sunday."

"Doing what?"

"Cleaning cages and feeding the dogs at the animal hospital."

"You have any hassles at work?"

"Not that I remember."

"Okay. You remember the name of the animal hospital?"

I told him.

He took out a little notebook and wrote it down, then said, "You worked on your car lately?"

"Just changed the oil."

"Not the brake fluid?"

"No. Why?"

"You got any enemies?"

"Just the Greenville goons."

"Who are they?"

"Just some jerks who live in Greenville."

"Could they have tampered with your brakes?"

"I never let them get that close to my car."

"Do you know their names?"

"I call them Moe, Larry, and Curly."

He gave me a don't-fuck-with-me look and said, "That's helpful."

I said, "If I knew, I don't remember."

"Anyone else who doesn't like you?"

"There's this creepy deputy sheriff."

"What makes you think he doesn't like you?"

"I don't know. He's got this thing for my ma, for one, even though she doesn't like him. He's always hanging around our street—like he's doing speed traps, even though our street's a dead end and there's only four houses on it. So who's he gonna catch?"

"I see. He said anything to you about your mother?"

"Yeah. He said he thinks she needs looking after."

Rhiann

The night before he went back home, Steve stayed at my house. After dinner, I lit candles, and we stayed up late drinking wine and reminiscing. Steve rolled a joint, and lit it.

"How did Mickey slip past the rest of us?" Steve asked.

I smiled to cover the remembered sadness. "Smoke was gone. Billy was MIA. You were so needy…I needed stability. Mickey was there. I didn't recognize the thousand-yard stare when I first saw him. I thought he was exotic. He was as troubled as Smoke, but he didn't let me see it. He was always my rock."

Steve took a long drag and passed the joint to me.

"The day he was killed he woke me up singing 'You Are My Sunshine.'" I sucked in the sweet smoke and passed the joint back.

Steve took a long drag and let his breath out slowly. He looked sad. "We loved you even before Smoke told us about

Rhiannon's birds singing to lure men."

Billy and Steve.

"But I always turned you down."

"Yeah, but you never made it hurt."

I smiled. "I never thought about it before, but how did Smoke know about Celtic mythology?"

"Probably read about it."

"Smoke?"

Steve grinned. "Yeah. He made me swear never to tell, but he used to hang out at the library—the times he ran away. I think Mrs. Hammond knew about his old man. And she used to let him stay there—even overnight sometimes. She paid him to shelve books and stuff so he could afford to go to McDonald's when his old man was on a tear and he couldn't go home. If you spend enough time in a library, you're bound to learn something."

"But why pretend to be ignorant…"

"Maybe he was afraid it would get back to his old man. *He* never got past the fifth grade and he was damned if his son would do better."

"I had such a crush on Smoke, I'd've put out for him if he'd ever asked me—he never did."

"Except that once."

I felt a stab of—What? Panic?

Steve smiled wryly. "After his mother died. Don't worry. I never told anyone."

"Did *he* tell you?"

Steve gave me his are-you-crazy? look. "Smoke? Never. I saw him leave your house the next morning. The way you kissed him, the way he looked, I knew."

• • •

Shortly before midnight, Smoke had scratched on my window. "Rhiann, you awake?"

I opened it and pulled him inside. He lowered the shade and slid his boots off. I lit the candles that I kept in my room for mood. We sat on the edge of my bed, and I tucked one foot under me. Smoke sat cross-legged, facing me. He looked around the room but didn't comment. It wasn't as if he'd never seen it. I'd sneaked him and Steve and Billy up many times when my folks weren't home.

He glanced at me and reddened, then looked away. "Nice nightgown."

It was a thin cotton floral print, sleeveless and scoop-necked, that came below my knees. I felt myself flush with pleasure, felt a pleasant sensation in my breasts. And lower. "It's okay to look," I told him.

"But not to touch." He looked everywhere but at me, which made me want to *make* him look.

I put my hands in my lap, pulling the slack out of the gown's front. I knew my nipples showed through the thin material. "It's okay for *you* to touch."

He got even redder. I'd never seen him scared, but he looked wary. "I didn't come here to make out."

"What *did you* come for?"

"To say good-bye."

"Where are you going?"

"I'll let you know when I get there."

"When're you coming back?"

"When I get here." He grinned at his own cleverness.

"Take me."

"Can't. Your folks'd have the National Guard out looking for us. And anyway, I can't support you yet."

Yet! Smoke didn't use words carelessly. That "yet" was the first clue he'd ever given me that I was other than a pal. I said, "Do you have to go now?"

He glanced at me again and shuddered and said, "Yeah, I do."

I grabbed hold of his shirt. "Kiss me good-bye."

He hesitated. I gave him my most imploring look. He leaned forward and pressed his lips against mine.

I was still a virgin, but I'd read plenty of romances. I opened my mouth a little and slid my tongue against his lips. I rubbed my palm against his fly. I could tell by the way he responded that I was getting something right.

He pulled away; I leaned forward to kiss him again.

He said, "If you keep that up I won't be able to stop."

"So?"

Later, when I was lying against the curve of his shoulder, feeling more contented than any time in my life, I had to ask. "Have you ever done that before?"

"Sure. Lots of times."

I jabbed his ribs with my elbow. "You lie!"

He laughed. "I've been saving myself for you." He squeezed me tighter; I got the feeling that he was only kidding a little. "But if you tell anyone I said so, I'll deny it."

We dozed off. He woke me when he bent over to kiss me good-bye.

"Don't go."

"I gotta. Your dad'll have my balls if he catches us." He kissed me again. "Your reputation's safe with me. I promise."

His exit wasn't as dramatic as the one in *Romeo and Juliet*, though he returned three times to give me one last kiss. The third time he even climbed back in my window. When he disappeared through the back hedge, I finally got the point of that sappy line in the movie about "parting" and "sorrow."

"Why did he go?" I asked Steve. "Not because of that?"

"Nah. I gave him a ride to the bus station. He told me he had to leave or he'd end up killing his old man."

"But forever?"

"He came back twice—after you and Billy got hitched. Then for Billy's memorial."

"I didn't see him."

"You weren't seeing much then. And after Billy was declared KIA, Mickey was always around, protecting you."

"I wish I'd known."

"You mean Billy and Mickey just got you on the rebound?"

I thought about how to answer truthfully but kindly. "Billy wanted me. And I didn't not want him."

"So maybe it's best he didn't come back."

"Billy?"

Steve nodded.

"No! I grew into love with Mickey. And he was the love of my life. I think it would have been the same with Billy." I took the joint from Steve and had another hit. "I wish they could've found something—a bone, a tooth, a boot—

something more than his knife and dog tags to prove he didn't just vanish in the Twilight Zone."

"There's Jimmy."

"He looks like me. But he was always Mickey's kid. Maybe not genetically, but Mickey's mannerisms, his morals. There's nothing of Billy in him."

"Billy was a good man." Steve took another drag. "But Mickey was almost a saint."

"It's sweet of you to say that. I know you weren't a big fan of his."

"Just jealous is all."

Jimmy

Bein' in the hospital is real boring. They have TVs in the room, but most of the time—'specially during the day—there's nothin' on worth watching. I couldn't explore the hospital 'cause I was in traction. I tried to read, but it gave me a headache. Mostly I just slept—when I could—and listened to the Walkman John brought me.

One day, I don't know how long after the accident—which I still couldn't remember—I asked the nurse if I could get a phone in my room.

"That's up to your mother," she said. "She'd be responsible for the bill."

I couldn't ask Ma—not that she wouldn't let me—'cause I'd have to tell her why. Which is why I was really glad to see Finn when he showed up after school.

He was carrying my backpack—the one I haul my books

in, back and forth to school. He dropped it next to the bed and sank into the visitor's chair.

"Finn, do me a favor."

"What, man?"

"I gotta get in touch with my girl. She's probably going nuts wondering what happened to me."

"Not if your ma told your boss what happened."

"Holy shit! I bet she didn't even think of that."

"Well, why don't *you* call him?"

I pointed to my strung-up leg and said, "*Duh.* Would you call him for me? Tell him what happened? Ask him to tell Beth?"

"Yeah, all right. But why don't I just call *her*?"

"I don't have her number."

"What do you think directory assistance is for?"

"I don't know her last name."

"You been goin' with this girl all summer and you don't know her name?"

"It's complicated."

"It's fuckin' nuts! What's the animal hospital number?"

"I can't remember."

Finn walked out of the room shaking his head.

When he came back, he looked even more confused.

"Well?" I said.

"Your boss thought you didn't show up 'cause you'd had a fight with Beth."

"Didn't she tell him?"

"She told him she didn't know *where* you were. But he

said she's been really moody, so he figured the two of you broke up, and she was just bummed about it."

"Swell. Why didn't he call my house?"

"He did, but he didn't get an answer, so he figured you'd just quit."

"Damn it!"

"Don't worry. When I told him what happened, he said to tell you, just get well. He's keepin' your job open for you."

"What about Beth?"

"She wasn't there. But he said he'd tell her what happened. Oh, and I got her number for you." Finn dangled a piece of paper over the bed, just out of reach. "What's it worth to you?"

"Give it to me and I won't kill you when I get outta here."

Rhiann

I was visiting my son after work one day, watering an azalea someone sent him, when his doctor came in to check the leg. At the end of the exam, he told Jimmy, "Three more weeks, you can go home."

Jimmy was already in a bad mood. John had told him his car was totaled. He promised he'd help Jimmy find another, but—he told me later—it wouldn't be the car his father gave him.

As soon as the doctor left, he demanded, "What am I gonna do in here for three more weeks?"

"Homework?"

"That's not funny, Ma."

One of the nurses poked her head into the room, preventing further discussion. "Are you up for a visitor?"

Jimmy looked at her suspiciously. He'd told me about his interview with the state investigator.

"She says she's your girlfriend," the nurse added.

"Beth?"

"She didn't give her name."

"Well, if it's Beth, sure."

The nurse disappeared. He ran his fingers through his hair "Ma, how do I loo—"

A very attractive blond girl interrupted when she came shyly through the doorway. "Jimmy?"

He practically bounced on the bed, held down only by the pully system keeping his leg in traction. A blind man could have seen his excitement.

"Beth" seemed reassured by Jimmy's reaction. She looked back toward the nurses' station, then crossed the room in two strides and threw herself on him.

Neither of them paid any attention to me. I'm sure Jimmy had forgotten I was there. Beth hadn't noticed.

"Oh, my God, Jimmy!" she said "What happened?"

"I totaled my car and broke my leg."

I smiled. He certainly had things in proper perspective. And it seemed to take her breath away.

"I was afraid the goons got you," she said.

"Nah."

I wondered who "the goons" were.

"I was afraid..." Beth went on. She swallowed. She looked around the room as if she might find the words she needed. She noticed me and seemed shocked.

"What?" Jimmy demanded.

"I thought after..." She took a deep breath. "I was afraid you'd changed your mind about me." She glanced at me as if gauging my reaction.

He looked hurt, then seemed to remember I was there. He turned red. "Don't be stupid," he told the girl. "Ma," he said to me, "this is my girlfriend, Beth."

John

I didn't see much of Rhiann the next week. She was back at work days, visiting the kid in the hospital evenings.

Wednesday, she forgot to put out her garbage. I knew they never locked the garage, so I let myself in and hauled the cans out to the curb. After the waste hauler emptied them, I put them back. On Thursday, I noticed her grass hadn't been touched for a while. When I cut my grass, I cut hers, too. By Friday, I was jonesing for the sight of her, for the sound of her voice. I could've hugged the mailman when she left the Faheys' phone bill in my mailbox.

Rhiann got home after nine, and I watched the lights go on and off as she made her way through the house. She only spent minutes in the kitchen—must have eaten at the hospital. The living room lights went back on, and I went across and rang the front doorbell.

When the door opened, I said, "Hi. How's Jimmy?"

I thought she looked tired, but maybe a little happy to see me. She said, "He's mending. I guess your prayers helped."

I let that go and offered her the phone bill. "Special delivery. I wish I could be Ed McMahon." When that didn't even get a smile, I added, "You're tired. I'll come back and make lame jokes another time."

She said, "Don't go." I waited. "Please come in. I—I need company. You're the only friend I've got."

"What about Steve?"

"He wants me too much."

As if I didn't. I went in. I didn't want to take advantage, but if she needed something…

She closed the door and stepped closer, tentatively. She put a hand on my chest, slid it up to my shoulder. I leaned a little toward her.

Then she took my face between her hands and kissed me.

I kissed her back, thinking that if I met her need, she might come in time to need *me*.

She thrust her hands under my jacket, behind my back, beneath my belt. She thrust against me and her breath came fast.

I could scarcely stand, but I had to ask, "Do you have protection?"

"Do you have something contagious?"

I pulled away—the hardest thing I've ever done. "That's not something you should ever take a man's word for."

That scarcely slowed her.

I said, "Wait here."

"I can't. Wait."

I backed away and headed for the door. She needed time to think; I needed a cold shower and my head examined.

I was walking better by the time I got to the Jeep. The Trojan box was still in the glove compartment. I grabbed a handful and headed back.

She hadn't locked the door. She was waiting where I'd

left her, leaning against the wall, hugging herself, rocking.

I knew it wasn't me she wanted. But I'd wanted her since I first saw her. I was content to have what I could get.

We tore the clothes off one another and sank onto the floor.

I barely got the rubber on before she was on top of me, and I was in. She rode me till I thought I would explode. Then, at the last minute, she rolled us over, clinging to me with hands and legs like we were welded together. She planted her feet against the floor and arched her back and screamed, "Come, please. Come!"

I felt as if all my life had been aimed toward this perfect moment.

Afterward, I rolled on my side to keep from crushing her. She stayed with me, resting her head on my arm. Every cell in my body had relaxed. The air in the room was chilly. Rhiann's body and her breath against my chest were hot in contrast. But we no longer fit together as perfectly as at the climax. I could feel myself slipping away from her. She acknowledged the loss with a little sigh.

I began to notice the rough fiber of the rug beneath me, the plastic surface of the urethane floorboards against my feet. I reached to retrieve the spent condom and felt for my shirt to wrap it in.

She kissed my chest and whispered, "Thank you." Then she sat up. Silhouetted against the dim light spilling through the window from a distant streetlight, she said, "Let's go upstairs."

I didn't trust my voice. I nodded.

She stood and tugged me to my feet. I felt around for the unused Trojans, then I followed her.

She led me to a room with a dresser, bedside table, and double bed, a guest room, I surmised—too clean to be the kid's, too small and impersonal for the room she'd shared with Mickey. She lit a candle and turned down the bed. She led me to it and sat me on the edge. She knelt between my knees. There was a sort of sadness in her movements; I had a déjà vu of the first girl I ever bedded.

We made love slowly, gently this time. She was newly widowed, still with Mickey; and I knew better than to compete with Mickey's shade. It was a *ménage à quatre*. We each brought an old love to the tryst, which should have made a crowd but didn't.

She opened to me in almost every way a woman could. She begged me to come in, to come. How could I refuse her anything?

I wanted to tell her that I loved her. That I had always loved her. And that I always would. But I was scared that I would frighten her, or that she'd see me as another Rory Sinter.

I had time. I gave her what she needed. I played the rock in a landscape of quicksand.

And if it wasn't perfect, it was good enough.

Rhiann

I came to my senses beside a perfect stranger—perfect because he was beautiful and too good to be true. I felt a tiny pang of guilt. Mickey had been dead less than half a year. But Mickey left me alone and grieving. He wouldn't have begrudged me the relief.

I looked at the naked man asleep beside me. He lay on his back. The slightly bemused expression he habitually wore had vanished. In the candlelight, he seemed younger. And sad. His white hair had fallen on his forehead, his perfectly trimmed beard looked gray in the candlelight.

I had never seen him without a shirt before, not even when he was cutting the grass on the hottest days. The tiny white scars on his forearms extended to his shoulders—he must have worn sleeveless shirts to weld. A line of dark fur ran down his torso to his belly button. His lower body was hidden by the sheet. But for the scars, he might have been a male model.

I kissed his shoulder, and he rolled over, with his back toward me. So I could see the other scars. And the tattoo.

I pulled the cover down. I recognized the archangel Michael on his back—a brooding guardian, stretching down his right side from his shoulder to his upper thigh. It wasn't the dashing hero from the stained-glass windows, but a more brooding saint. The snake curled round his feet was dead, head pierced by a Samurai sword. The angel's expression was guarded, and a single tear graced its right cheek. Beneath the figure, John's skin was striped with whiter scars. As were his thighs and butt cheeks.

He came awake suddenly. I could see him start, then relax as he remembered where he was. He rolled over smiling.

His smile faded as he focused on my face. "What's the matter?"

"Why is the angel crying?"

He rolled onto his back, pulling the sheet up to his waist. He stared at the ceiling. "It's a long story."

"Is that a polite way of saying 'none of your business'?" I was propped up on one elbow facing him. I lay back, shoving my right arm under the pillow so I could watch him comfortably.

"No. I let you see the tattoo. I guess you have a right to ask about it."

I waited.

He said, "I went to prison when I was nineteen. I'd been in trouble before, but never in jail. It's a rough place for a kid. I knew enough to keep my back to the wall and act mean—a sympathetic deputy warned me to do that. But nothing prepared me for the constancy. Guys join gangs in stir just to have someone to watch their backs. I didn't want to do that, so I tried to go it alone. Pretty soon I wasn't acting. I had a hair-trigger temper, and was psychotic for lack of sleep."

I tried to imagine him at nineteen—just two years older than Jimmy, trapped with gangbangers and pedophiles. I shivered.

John didn't seem to notice. "I've always read a lot. I noticed the prison library was quiet and there was never any trouble in there, so I started spending as much time there as they'd let me. I was supposed to be researching my appeal. I wasn't planning to appeal, but I *did* research—for other inmates. I made friends with the librarian, Carl, an old guy doing three life sentences for murder. He'd been in for thirty-eight years. I must've reminded him of himself." John shrugged. "For whatever reason, he took me under his wing. Gave me pointers on how to get by, let me sleep when there was no one else around. He encouraged me to get my GED and to draw."

John reached around and felt his back, where the angel's head faced into the sheet beneath him. "I drew this one day—the guardian angel I wished I had. One of the worst bullies in the cell block happened to see it and started ragging me about it. So I told him it was a design for a tattoo I was planning on getting. That shut him up for a while, but when we had a jailhouse tattoo artist transferred to the wing, I had to let him have a crack at it. He did a pretty good job—made the face just eerie enough to freak out anybody sneaking up behind me in the shower. I started telling people my guardian angel had my back, and pretty soon I had a rep for having eyes in the back of my head. There were enough superstitious idiots who believed me and spread the word, so pretty soon the guys were leaving me alone."

John stole a glance at me, and I touched his arm to let him know I wasn't put off by his story. He went back to staring at the ceiling.

But he hadn't answered my question. "Why is the angel crying?"

"A fight broke out in the cafeteria one night, just before my release. Carl tried to break it up and got shanked for his trouble. I grabbed the guy who did it and nearly beat him to death before the guards showed up. Oddly enough, no one ratted on me. To a man, they said my victim fell down and hurt himself.

"It was obvious Carl wasn't going to make it. They let me stay with him. I was too close to breaking down to talk, so I made a tear on my face with his blood—Here..." John put a finger to his cheek below the outer corner of his eye.

"Where the bangers put tattoos to mark their fallen homies. The last thing he did before he died was grab my hand and say, 'Don't brand yourself a con. Swear it.' After I got out, I had a professional redo the tattoo and put the tear on the angel's face. For Carl."

"Could I see it again?"

He rolled on his side. I moved the candle for a better look.

The figure was skillfully drawn with black lines and blue and purple shading—an Art Deco comic book hero in Levi's, with traditional wings, a Samurai sword and a garbage can lid for a shield. Somehow the odd elements fit together.

I had to touch it. John's skin was warm, and he flinched as if it tickled. I pulled the sheet down to see the angel's feet. The serpent curled around them was a giant diamondback. The candlelight brought the figure to life and raised the scars surrounding it in bas relief.

I pulled the sheet back up and put the candle on the night-stand. "Did you get the scars in prison, too?"

"No." His tone made it clear the scars were not a subject he'd discuss. He reached over me to pinch the candle out. He lowered his weight onto me, as he whispered in my ear: "Let's talk about something else."

John

The next morning, I left Rhiann sleeping and went in to work an hour before anyone else was due to show up. I needed time to think.

Didn't get it. A state police car was parked in front of my

shop when I got there. The driver was reading a newspaper, but he spotted my Jeep and put the paper down as I pulled up. When he rolled his window down, I recognized Sergeant Crowley.

I got out and walked over to lean against the car. "What can I do for you this morning, Sergeant?"

He got out and leaned against the front fender. He folded his arms. "I haven't gotten too much cooperation from Jimmy Fahey. I was wondering if you could help me out."

I shrugged. "If I can."

"He works for you."

"Yes."

"He have problems with anyone here?"

"Not that I'm aware of. He's a pretty friendly kid. Modest. Helpful. Most of my guys appreciate that."

"Most?"

"A couple don't care one way or another."

Crowley wasn't taking notes, but I got the impression he wouldn't miss or forget anything. "He work on his own car?"

"Yes."

"What kind of work?"

I wasn't sure what he was getting at, so I just went with the truth. "Oil changes, filter replacements, tire rotations—simple stuff. I helped him with more complicated things."

"Such as?"

"Carburetor adjustments. Timing."

"He ever do a brake job?"

"Not here."

Crowley nodded. "He ever tell you what he does on weekends?"

"He didn't spell it out, but I gather he got his weekend

job to be close to his girlfriend."

"He tell you about her?"

"Said she's 'perfect,' and that her father won't let her date." Apparently, that hadn't put a damper on their relationship, but I left it to Crowley to discover that for himself.

"He tell you about any problems he had with anyone in Greenville?"

"Just that he had a couple run-ins with some football players from Greenville High—bullies he tries to avoid."

"You think they sabotaged his brakes?"

"Whoever did this just loosened the bleeder screw. Right?"

Crowley nodded. "Unsophisticated but effective."

"From what Jimmy said, I gather they'd be more likely to take baseball bats to his car."

"The Alva police tell me you're a poster child for the Illinois correctional system."

I waited for his point.

When I didn't respond to that, he added, "So maybe you could help me out."

"How's that?"

"I gotta interview those football players. Don't have their names, but I got information that the car they drive recently suffered some rear-end damage. There was a police report, so it shouldn't be too hard to run them down. I thought maybe you'd like to get in on the interview."

"Why me?"

"You got a rep for being good with cars and tough kids. And you got an interest in seeing this thing solved."

"What about your hypothetical defense lawyer?"

Crowley shrugged. "I don't necessarily have to mention

you in my report. And if nobody asks, neither of us has to tell."

I hadn't been to Greenville in years. The last time was on business, and I was driving. No time for sightseeing. Riding shotgun with Crowley gave me the chance to really look.

The city hall and library were vintage but the high school was new and big, with a billboard in front advertising the football team. No mention of chess or drama, or National Merit Scholarships.

We stopped at the police station—renovated inside—so Crowley could give the locals a heads-up and get a copy of the police report.

Back in the car, he said it didn't add much to what he'd gotten through channels. "Mrs. Fahey told me her son works for the local veterinarian. Maybe we should talk to him before we go to the school—see if he can give us the name of Jimmy's girlfriend."

"He didn't tell you?"

"Said he couldn't remember. He tell you?"

"Beth. He didn't mention her last name."

"Well, we need one. So let's go talk to the doctor."

Rhiann

John was gone when I awoke. I lay for a long time, trying to sort through the mare's nest of feelings overwhelming me.

Last night had been orgasmic, a bonding, a replay of almost-remembered events. I felt relief that John was gone. Gratitude that he'd come last night. Hope. Fear of another abandonment. Confusion. That maddening sense that I'd lived this moment earlier and forgotten it.

I lay very still, willing the feeling to condense into something I could grasp.

And then I had it.

After months of unofficial courtship, I felt a huge sense of loss the first morning Mickey didn't come in for breakfast. I'd gotten used to seeing him. By lunch, I was near tears and so out of sorts that Henry told me to go home.

"PMS ain't good for business."

I used my upset up on housework. By suppertime, the house was spotless, Jimmy bathed and fed. And I was asking myself—for the umpteenth time, How could he do this to me? Playing the devil's advocate, too: He never promised you a rose garden. Or even a bush.

Mickey showed up as I was putting Jimmy to bed. Ma let him in and sent him up to Jimmy's room. Mickey was the first man in my life that Ma truely approved of.

"Did you miss me?" he asked—only half kidding, I'd've bet.

"Why do you ask?"

He looked disappointed.

"I did," Jimmy chimed in.

"I missed you, too," Mickey told him, though I think he was speaking to me, as well.

"Read me a story?" Jimmy said.

"That's why I came." Mickey gave me a so-there look. "Which one?"

"*Harold and the Purple Crayon*. It's my favorite."

"My favorite, too," Mickey assured him.

After the story, Mickey kissed Jimmy good night and left me to tuck him in.

Mickey was waiting in the living room, visiting with Ma when I came down.

Ma looked from him to me and said, "I think I'll make coffee. Anyone want any?"

I shook my head. Mickey said, "No, thanks," and Ma disappeared.

Mickey looked at me and asked, seriously, "Did you miss me?"

I looked at him for a long time before I said, "Yes."

He nodded as if that was the right answer. "I was applying for a job."

"Did you get it?"

"Yeah."

"Tell me."

"I want to ask you something first."

That made me suspicious. "What?"

"Will you marry me?"

It wasn't what I expected, but I said, "Yes!" without hesitation. He'd set me up with Harold and by kissing Jimmy good night. "Tell me about the job."

"I won't take it if you don't want me to."

"Tell me!"

"I got accepted by the state police."

I knew instantly that I was marrying another soldier,

that I could be widowed again at any time. But I could see how much the job meant to him. I threw my arms around him and squeezed with all my strength.

"Mickey, that's wonderful!"

The office was twenty minutes from our house and, though I didn't have a set starting time, I usually got to work by eight. Frank was always in before me. Today was no exception. He glanced up when I came through the door and said, "Good morning."

"Good morning, Frank."

I think he did a double take: I wasn't paying close attention. He said, "You're chipper this morning."

"It's a beautiful morning."

He looked out the window as if he might've missed something coming in. "It's gonna rain."

"My roses will be so happy."

"You been drinking?"

"No, Frank. I'm just high on life."

He was quiet for a moment, regarding me suspiciously. Then he said, "You've fallen for Devlin, haven't you?" From the look on his face, he'd guessed that we'd gotten as far as sleeping together.

In spite of his disappearance this morning, John still seemed too good to be true. I wasn't sure I knew him or if I was just infatuated with some idealized stranger, if what I felt was love, or just relief from loss and loneliness.

But Frank was so different from John or Mickey, almost timid. I didn't see my feelings for Frank changing. Ever. So

I said, "Yes, Frank."

"He could be dangerous—there's something about him. I can feel it."

I could feel it, too, in the quiet confidence he projected. He could be dangerous but… "He means me no harm."

"For now."

"Now is all I have, Frank. Mickey's death taught me that."

John

Dr. Pulaski's appraisal of Jimmy was pretty much like mine: "Good kid. Hard worker. Nuts about Beth." Beth's last name? "Wilding."

I wondered how closely she was related to the birth father Jimmy'd mentioned. Not out loud. Not my place to bring it up.

By the time we finished at the vet's, it was nearly noon. We headed for the school.

"Miss Wilding is home sick today." The Greenville High School principal so reminded me of the man who'd held the post at *my* high school that I wondered if there was a factory somewhere mass-producing them. "I can give you her home phone number, but you'll have to get her parents' permission to interrogate her."

Crowley kept his cool. "Miss Wilding isn't a suspect, but she may be able to help us in the investigation of a serious crime."

"What crime?"

"I'm not at liberty to say."

"Well, I'm sorry. I can't help you."

I said, "How about her girlfriends?" All high school girls had girlfriends. "Maybe one of them could help us?"

"I wouldn't know—"

"Her homeroom teacher would."

"I can't ask—"

Crowley interrupted. "You wouldn't want to be seen as impeding a police investigation."

"Ah...No."

"Good." Crowley waited.

The principal finally picked up his phone. "Barbara, go and send Miss Amberly to the office. And keep an eye on her class until she returns."

When Miss Amberly arrived, Crowley thanked the principal for his cooperation, and for the use of his office for our interviews.

Miss Amberly was quite concerned about the police interest in her students; Crowley immediately set her at ease. Miss Wilding was under no suspicion herself, but was friends with a student from another school who was recently injured in a serious accident. "We're hoping, since Miss Wilding is absent today, that one of her girlfriends might have information that would help us."

Miss Amberly gave a relieved sigh. "That would be Stephanie."

"She's here today?"

"I'll ask Barbara to locate her and send her in."

• • •

Stephanie was a nervous brunette, dressed a la mode. When Crowley asked her to have a seat, she looked as if she expected to be shot. "What's this about?"

"You're a friend of Beth Wilding?" he asked.

"Ye-es." Her eyes darted from Crowley to me and back.

"You know Jimmy Fahey?"

She relaxed slightly. "Is this about Jimmy's accident?"

"How do you know about that?"

"Beth told me."

"*What* did she tell you?"

"Just that he crashed his car and broke his leg and he couldn't call her because he's in the hospital in traction. Is he gonna be all right?"

"He'll live."

Stephanie relaxed a little more.

"You know anybody who'd want to hurt Fahey?"

Her eyes widened. "It wasn't an accident?"

"We're looking into that."

"The goons!"

Crowley waited; she elaborated, then said, "You think they ran him off the road?"

"Why would they do that?"

So she told us.

Crowley had Barbara pull the football players out of class one at a time so they wouldn't have a chance to confer on an alibi. Individually, they told us they'd been together the

Sunday night before Jimmy's crash, watching a game on TV. Under pressure, they admitted to getting too wasted to drive home. They'd spent the night together and showed up hungover at school the next day. Their coach confirmed the hangovers.

About Jimmy Fahey, the three bullies agreed: He was a fast-talking asshole who fought dirty and had given them trouble on several occasions. The last time they'd seen him, he'd gotten them ticketed for speeding.

"How does that work?" Crowley asked the kid who got the ticket.

"He got us to chase him, then lured us into a speed trap."

"*He* didn't get caught?"

"Nah. I think he was in cahoots with the cop. He went around a curve and pulled over, so we got nailed."

"What makes you think he wasn't just lucky?"

"'Cause the cop was real nasty—like he was pissed at us. But we never saw him before, so he must've been a friend of Fahey's getting us back for giving him grief."

"Did you?"

"What?"

"Give him grief?"

"Never really got the chance."

"You didn't beat him up at the Dairy Queen?"

"Before we could touch him, the manager came after us with a baseball bat."

"What was the name of the cop that gave you the ticket?"

The kid shrugged.

"You still got the ticket?"

"Nah—went to court on it already."

"And?"

"I got supervision. But it cost me a hundred bucks."

"What department was this cop with?"

"Sheriff's police."

"What'd he look like?"

"Mean."

Crowley threw a look at me and asked him, "Who works on your car?"

The kid looked annoyed. "What's this about?"

"Just a question."

"I take it to Marv's Garage. On Western."

I asked, "You change your own oil?"

He gave me a withering look, "Why would I?"

I shrugged. "Some guys like to."

"Grease monkeys."

I asked him a few more questions. His answers made it clear that putting gas in his tank was an intellectual challenge. Crowley thanked him for his help and told him he could go.

"What do you think?" Crowley asked me when we were back on the road.

"If I were a betting man, I'd put money on Sinter being the sheriff's cop who issued that ticket."

"You think he figured out that Jimmy suckered those guys into the speed trap?"

"Ah huh. And I'll bet he works on his own brakes."

Jimmy

I still saw Ma every day in the hospital, but being there, I realized how much I missed John and Steve and Beth.

Especially Beth. But it had an upside.

Finn came by every day with my homework—which he helped me with, and we'd shoot the shit. I'd missed that during the summer.

He caught me up on things at school, and how he and Ali were doing.

I told him I planned to marry Beth.

And we tried to figure out why my brakes failed.

"Maybe someone cut your brake line."

"I think the cops would've noticed. They're usually all over that kind of thing when there's an accident."

"You ask John about it?"

"I didn't think to. But I will."

John

When I went to answer the bell the next night, I didn't recognize the guy standing with his back to the door. He had on a cowboy hat, denim jacket, and jeans. The truck idling in the driveway was equally unfamiliar—a middle-aged black Ford F-250 with a loaded gun rack. Fairly common in a town surrounded by farms. Thinking it might be someone lost, I opened the door.

Deputy Sinter turned and aimed his revolver at me. "I got a warrant."

I said nothing.

He gestured for me to back up, and I retreated to my living room. Sinter followed, finger on the trigger. Bad technique, especially since his hand was shaking. He smelled of beer. He kicked the door closed behind him and looked around, turned his head to glance at the uncurtained windows flanking the entry.

"What do you want, Sinter?"

"You. Dead."

I waited.

"You fucked her, didn't you?"

"What would make you think that?"

"I saw you leave with her last week."

"She left her car at work. I gave her a ride home and back to the hospital."

I saw him think about that. He studied the room, then focused on the door in the east wall. "What's in there?"

"My office."

He gestured at it with the gun. "Get in there. Keep your hands where I can see 'em."

I went toward the office, though it made my hair stand up to turn my back on him. As soon as I turned the knob, he shoved me—hard.

I hit the door with my hands and face; it flew inward. I went down on hands and knees. Sinter landed a steel-toed boot on the back of my thigh. I rolled away. He followed, holstering his gun. He held his arms high for balance and landed kicks on my ribs and back.

He stopped suddenly.

His eyes stretched wide. His jaw sagged. His head swiveled as he took in the framed pictures on the walls—the last thing I wanted him to see.

I took the opportunity to scramble to my feet.

I could have taken his gun away, but disarming him would be a mortal insult. I wasn't prepared to kill him and I would have had to.

He must have studied the pictures a full minute. His face went white, then red. He came at me with his fists balled, his jaw clenched.

I blocked his worst blows, stopped the others with my fore-arms, ribs, and shoulders. He used me like a heavy bag, giving himself a proper workout.

I took it, waiting for his rage to fade, or for him to wear himself out.

I'd absorbed worse blows from far more murderous men.

Rhiann

I knew something bad was going to happen when I saw Rory Sinter's truck pull into John Devlin's drive. Rory's personal truck. Rory got out and went to the front door. He was wearing civilian clothes.

Instinct told me to call the cops, but what cops? Rory *was* the police in this neighborhood, and the sheriff had made it plain that he'd believe Rory. I went to where I'd put Mickey's gun.

The .38 was loaded—it wouldn't do much good in an emergency otherwise. I broke it open and checked the cylinder anyway. Then, with the gun down at my side, I hurried over to John's.

The front door was closed. I prayed it was unlocked. I listened before I touched the knob. No angry voices. I turned it; the door swung inward. I entered cautiously. The room was clean, attractively furnished, unoccupied.

But beyond a half-open door, there were sounds of the violence I'd expected. Sounds I remembered well from childhood, of fists striking flesh. A voice I recognized as Rory's was too angry to be understood, his snarl was like a dog's fighting. I ran across and slipped through the doorway.

The room I entered was obviously an office, with phone and computer on a polished wood desk, a matching credenza with fax machine and printer, filing cabinets. I took a shooter's stance, pointing Mickey's revolver at Rory.

He was standing in front of John, one fist clenched on John's shirt, the other aimed at John's face.

John was backed up to the desk, wearing a poker face and blood smears where Rory'd hit him. His hands hung at his sides.

I pulled the hammer back.

Rory heard the sound and paled. He glanced at me; he didn't let John go. "Your precious ex-con, here, is a fuckin' nut job!" He hitched his free thumb toward the wall behind him. "You two deserve each other."

Keeping the gun on him, I glanced around the room. The walls were covered with framed pictures—drawings and photos. Of me. Scary.

But one thing at a time, I told myself. Rory first.

I said, "Rory, get out. Now!"

He let go of John's shirt and sidled toward the door. "Happy to."

I kept the gun on him. "Rory, if you don't leave us alone, I'm going to announce in church on Sunday that you've been bothering me."

"And who'd believe that?"

"Your wife for one."

He stopped in the doorway. "Don't worry. You couldn't get me to *arrest* you if you were doin' ninety in a school zone." He looked at John. "But you better watch out."

John said nothing. Rory left. I kept the gun leveled at the doorway until we heard the front door slam and Rory's truck pull away. Then I let my gun hand drop to my side. John stayed where he was. I studied the room.

There must've been a hundred pictures. Pictures of me alone. Pictures of me watching Mickey and Jimmy. Pictures of me at home, and coming out of church. In my car. At work. At Jimmy's games at school. Even a picture taken at Mickey's funeral.

I turned around and pointed the gun at John. "What the hell is this about?"

He seemed more sad than scared.

"I love you, Rhiann. I've always loved you."

I looked back at the pictures. "How long…?"

"Since the first time I saw you."

"When was that?"

"The day I put the frog down your dress."

I could feel my face slacken with disbelief. The gun sagged floorward. "Smoke?

"Impossible!" I added, reaiming the gun. "Smoke's dead." I pulled back the hammer. "Did you kill him?"

He looked surprised, then thoughtful, then sad again. "I guess in a way I did."

I was shaking with rage, which must have been obvious.

He held his hands up, fingers spread, and said, "Figuratively. Only figuratively."

As if to set me at ease, he backed up, folding his arms across his chest. He parked his butt against the edge of the desk. The action was reassuring enough to make me relax a tiny bit.

"Smoke died," he said, "the day of Amy Johnson's funeral."

Smoke had been a pallbearer, solemn in his black suit, carefully ignoring the father seated—half-lit—in the front church pew, then in the front row at the cemetery.

As they lowered the casket, Smoke was stone-faced. Mourners shuffled past, tossing their handsful of dirt onto the coffin, reciting their platitudes, or, when even clichés failed, hugging the family members. Steve and Billy and I waited till the end, hoping to take Smoke someplace quiet and safe.

When I hugged him, Smoke almost smiled. He'd wiped away my tears—shed for him. I hadn't known his mother.

I'd moved on to let the others offer comfort, when his old man staggered up. He clapped Smoke on the back and said, "Well, it's just you and me, kid."

I could see Smoke fight to control himself. He turned his back on his father and told me, "See you later." Then he stalked away across the graveyard. His old man swayed drunkenly, staring after him.

"What's with Smoke?" Billy'd asked me later. He looked uncomfortable in his dress uniform. Home on bereavement leave, though Amy Johnson hadn't been his kin.

"He's hurting," Steve said. "Let him be."

• • •

I kept the gun steady. "Who the hell *are* you?"

He didn't answer. I moved toward him until the muzzle of the gun came up against his chest. He didn't seem to care, or even notice, really. I tried to imagine *this* man without a beard, with a crew cut and a few more pounds on his frame. I tried to imagine him going on eighteen and cocky. The resemblances were there, when you knew what to look for, but *something* was missing.

"If you're Smoke, tell me what you swore to me before you left town." He'd said, "I'll die before I tell anyone about us. I swear."

"I never told anyone. I've always kept my promises."

It had been a point of honor with Smoke. He'd rarely committed to anyone or anything, but if he did, he kept his word.

He'd never told me he'd come back to me.

"Why did you leave?"

"I told you that. I would've killed my old man if I stayed."

"Why didn't you take me with? Or come back for me?"

"I had no education, no skills, no job." He'd told me that, too. "I thought if we married, in ten or fifteen years I'd be my father, taking my failure out on you."

I shook my head and let the gun drop to my side. "That's crazy."

"Maybe. Seventeen-year-olds don't have much truck with logic. I did return, eventually, but you were married and expecting—Billy's kid. I came back again for Billy's memorial. You were with Mickey. I could see he was crazy about you and he really cared about the kid. It seemed better for everyone if I just left it there. No need to raise old ghosts."

Jimmy was two by then, and I'd resigned myself to Billy's loss. I took a step back. If only…

But Billy had pleaded his case on bended knee.

Mickey'd made it plain that he adored me and that he worshipped my son.

Smoke had braved my father's wrath to climb in through my bedroom window.

This shade of Smoke only waited. I felt bereaved again.

He said, "Rhiann, I'm sorry."

"For what?"

"Everything."

I looked around. The stalkerlike obsession seemed, suddenly, more pathetic than threatening. "You're right," I said. "You *did* manage to kill Smoke. He never would have apologized."

"He should have."

He didn't move as I cradled the gun in the crook of my arm and walked out of the room.

John

After Rhiann walked out of my life, I closed up the house and drove to my studio. I got out charcoal and the four-foot-by-four-foot newsprint pad and began to fill the pages. I tore each sheet off as it was filled and threw it aside. I didn't stop until I ran out of paper.

I was spent, too. I gathered up the sheets and stuffed them in the trash. Then I passed out on the cot I keep in the studio for all-nighters.

Rhiann

When Smoke left, I hadn't grieved. I'd accepted that he had his reasons and I'd just assumed that he'd return for me. Until I found that I was pregnant, I didn't even worry.

But weeks passed, and I began to show. Billy guessed and asked me to marry him. I loved Billy almost as much as I loved Smoke. And I hadn't heard from Smoke—or even anything about him. So I told Billy yes.

I thought of Smoke fondly. He'd left me with a gift. But as time went on, I thought of him less often. And after I married Mickey, not at all.

Now memories of Smoke filled my head. I locked my door and put Mickey's gun away. And I cried myself to sleep.

I slept fitfully, dreaming I was losing Mickey again.

I woke full of curiosity. And anger.

What could've made Smoke change so much I didn't know him? All the passion and humor and fun had drained out of him, leaving only a depressing sadness.

And what made Rory think he could get away with…? How far would he have gone?

John

When I awoke, around noon, I pulled the newsprint sheets out of the garbage and studied the angry, despairing images

I'd made the night before. Everything I couldn't articulate or didn't dare express, every murderous and suicidal impulse, lust and loss and longing, even the violent sexual urges Rhiann stirred in me had gone onto those sheets.

Enough venting. I started again, making my sketches on the white walls of the studio, tempering my passion with reflection. I tried to reify my loss—not just of Rhiann—my mother; Steve and Billy; Carl; the structure that my hatred of my father gave my life until he, too, ceased to be; and opportunities...

The gun was there. The revolver that she'd pointed at Sinter, then as seriously at me, morphed into the rifle Billy carried to Vietnam. Then I abstracted it.

I caught the look on Rhiann's face when she'd thought I'd killed Smoke literally. I abstracted that, as well.

The frog that symbolized so much between us over the years made its way into the design, a tiny corpse.

When I was satisfied with the sketches, I planned their execution, calculating the scope and the materials I'd need. That done, I called and left a message at the shop—that I'd be gone a while.

It hit me, then, that I hadn't eaten in a day. I wasn't hungry. I thought maybe if I went where I could smell food, I could eat something. I closed up the studio and got in my Jeep. Where to?

I'm not sure what impulse made me turn toward Greenville.

Rhiann

"Sheriff, Rory beat up my neighbor." I'd barged in past the deputy and entered the office without knocking.

Sheriff Linden hid whatever surprise he felt. "Good morning to you, too, Mrs. Fahey."

"Did you hear me?"

"I did. Is your neighbor in the hospital?"

"No."

"You an' him run off an' get married recently?"

"No, of course not."

"Well, then, if he's got a complaint against Rory, he'll have to come in an' make it himself."

"But I witnessed it!"

"If you had any sense, you'd realize Rory's just trying to protect you."

"Rory's a Peeping Tom. And he was coming on to me before John Devlin came to town."

"I think Devlin's got you razzle-dazzled. But I don't care how much money he's got, or even if he's got talent, far as I'm concerned, he's a convicted killer."

"What makes you think John's got money?"

My surprise must have shown on my face, because the sheriff snorted. "Rory did a background check. Devlin's art collection alone's got to be worth a million or two."

My surprise became amazement. "He didn't tell me he collects art."

"He doesn't collect it, he makes it. You didn't know?" I shook my head.

"I know he's a good neighbor and a great mechanic."

• • •

As soon as I left the sheriff's office, I drove to the Overlook Public Library and called Frank to beg off work. I had too many questions to keep my mind on business.

Who was John Devlin really? When did the Frog Prince become an artist? And for that matter, what sort of art did a mechanic make? I had to know.

The library had a reference librarian who reminded me of Mrs. Hammond. "How do you find out about someone?" I asked her.

"What, exactly, do you want to know?"

"Whether someone has a wife and kids, or a prison record, or owns real estate."

"Well, let's start with the easiest. Property. The county assessor may be able to tell you if someone owns property. Contact City Hall about a business or the state incorporation registry. About a prison record—you'll have to contact the police."

"Thank you. I also need to research an artist named John Devlin."

She went right to work. Five minutes later, she said, "I believe you're in luck. Mr. Devlin has an exhibit in Chicago."

Steve opened the door and saw me and did a double take. "Rhiann, come in."

The place wasn't much different from my childhood memories. Aunt Emily had kept it neater, but the same family pictures covered the wall opposite the front door, the same *Readers' Digests* and *National Geographies* spilled off the coffee table. If the couch was new, it had been chosen for its resemblance to the one it replaced. New rug, new drapes; no different in style than those I remembered. Everything comfortably familiar. Like Steve.

"Okay," he said, when I was planted on the couch. "What's up?"

"Smoke's alive."

"No," he said.

"He lives next door to me. John Devlin."

He gave me a disgusted look. "That guy's just a ghost."

I started to protest. Steve held up a hand. "He looked me up at Hannigan's last night. I'm having a game of darts when I hear this familiar voice say, 'How's it going, Steve?' I think, *A voice from the past!*

"So I say, 'Smoke!' I whip around and there's Devlin.

"An' *he* says, 'Once. Long ago.' An' now he *sounds* like Devlin.

"I take a good look. And it's him—sorta. I say, 'Fifteen years you let us think you're dead.' Then I deck him—split his lip open. He doesn't even hit back. Smoke would—in a heartbeat. No way he'd let anybody get away with that. This guy just gets up and stands there, like he's waiting for me to hit him again—didn't even raise his hands. Denny almost throws us out. I had to convince him it was just a joke.

"Then this guy—I can't think of him as Smoke—Devlin offers to buy me a drink and explain." Steve shrugged. "What could I do?

"He gives me this cockamamy story about how he was in prison and then got out and straightened out his life. And how he's now a famous sculptor."

"He said famous?"

"Well, successful."

"He is. Very. He gets upwards of thirty thousand for a small piece."

"Yikes! What about the prison thing?"

I nodded. "Rory Sinter made a point to tell me John has a record."

"So it's all true?"

I shrugged.

"But there's something wrong with the guy. He's not Smoke. So we come back to where we started—Smoke's dead."

"So it would appear. What did he say about me?"

"Just that he loves you, but you're not interested. That true?"

I wasn't sure. I said, "Smoke's gone. And I don't know John Devlin. I thought I did. I thought he was this nice, ordinary, helpful neighbor. He's turned out to be *not* ordinary, and I'm wondering about the nice and helpful."

Steve shook his head. "You should have chosen me back in sixth grade."

"*You* didn't put a frog down my dress."

John

Leaving Rhiann's the morning after my mother's funeral, after we first became lovers, was the hardest thing I'd done in my life. She loved me! And I'd felt as if no one ever would again.

I'd known I had to leave town. I would have killed the old man if I stayed. Now I didn't want to go. Couldn't.

I went back to the cemetery. Unlike the day before, it was peaceful—no well-meaning people reminding me my ma was dead with their condolences. No sign of the old man. Not even any ghosts, as far as I could tell—just trees and grass and headstones. And Ma's grave like a new scab on the green skin of the marble orchard. I went and lay down on the dew-wet grass next to it. Face up, I laced my fingers behind my head and stared at the sky, trying to hear Ma's voice telling me what to do. But the only sound was birds squabbling the way they do at first light. I fell asleep.

When I awoke, the birds had all left for work and the sun was burning my face. I sat up and tried to memorize the gravesite so I could find it again because I didn't think the old man would ever pop for a headstone. I checked out Ma's new neighbors who had stones with inscriptions like "Beloved Wife," "Loving Husband," and "Cherished Child."

Someday I'd buy Ma a stone that said "Amy Johnson/ Beloved Mother of—" Who? Tommy Johnson? He was my old man. As far as I could tell, he'd never "beloved" anyone, especially my mother. Smoke? I guess that was as true a name as I'd ever had. But people who knew me would say "Smoke Johnson, that asshole Tommy Johnson's kid."

As soon as I had that thought, I wanted to be someone else. Someone nobody associated with Tommy Johnson or his poor wife, Amy. I wanted to be someone beloved.

I was. By Rhiann. But she was still a kid, really, and I couldn't support her. Yet. I couldn't give her a name she could be proud of.

Then I spotted the child's grave: JOHN DEVLIN 1952-1954 BELOVED SON OF JOHN AND MARY DEVLIN. John and Mary Devlin had died in 1954, too, and were buried on either side of him. Son John had been born the same year as I. His stone wasn't huge or ostentatious, but it was decorated with smiling cherubs and the words "Angels Keep You."

There was a kid who could've been someone because his parents loved him. Well, my ma had loved me. But she was dead, turned into an actual angel.

I stood in front of the kid's stone and talked to him as if he could hear me. "I'm gonna borrow your name," I said. "And I'm gonna try'n make something of it."

Then I turned to Ma's grave and told her to watch out for the Devlin kid. "And watch out for me, too."

It wasn't hard to become John Devlin. I burned my driver's license and everything else with the name Smoke or Tommy Johnson on it. I went to the county building and told them I needed a copy of my birth certificate so I could get my driver's permit. I said my name was John Devlin and my parents were John and Mary Devlin, that I was born in 1952. They gave me a form to fill out and charged me fifteen dollars. And I walked out with a notarized copy of John Devlin's birth certificate. I've been John Devlin ever since.

Rhiann

John's retrospective was at the Museum of Contemporary Art in Chicago. I took the train to Union Station, then a

CTA bus to Michigan and Ontario. I walked the last two blocks. It was a perfect fall day. I hadn't been to the city since the day Billy and I were married. I was amazed at the changes. It seemed cleaner and brighter than I remembered.

I felt terribly sad. No. Lonely. Billy was gone. And Mickey. Smoke seemed to be gone for good, too—some part of him had died. Steve had drowned his potential in alcohol. Jimmy would be going to college soon, leaving me as alone in Overlook as I felt in this city of a million strangers.

As if to knock me out of my moody fit, a man hurrying along the sidewalk bumped me hard enough to make me stagger. He caught me before I fell and muttered, "Sorry," insincerely, before he charged away.

I muttered, "Clumsy," and checked to see that I still had my wallet.

The man stopped at the next corner and waved frantically at a cab.

I went into the museum.

The retrospective took up most of the first floor. Two huge abstract stone sculptures stood like sentries on either side of the exhibit entrance. The docent handed me a brochure, and I stepped between the giant stones. The brochure said the stones were on loan from a corporation I'd never heard of. Titled *Emergent Possibilities I* and *Emergent Possibilities II*, they seemed to be hatching polished curves and bulges from their rough granite sides. I didn't get them.

Farther along there were more stone pieces that seemed to invite me to feel their smooth surfaces. Most of them had DO NOT TOUCH signs, but one—*Hands On*—had PLEASE TOUCH chiseled under its face. And it *was* a face, with smooth cheeks, furrowed brows, and full, wrinkled lips. Its curls looked like the hair I'd seen in pictures of Greek statues. The face had a beard that felt just like a man's two-day-old stubble, though it just looked like a different-colored stone.

As I moved farther from the entrance, the sculptures became more realistic—a granite bear standing on three feet to scratch its chin with the fourth; a life-sized bronze horse prancing with head and tail held high; a cat carved from black walnut—the sign said—arching its back in an angry hiss. And a giant frog cut from green marble, polished until its skin seemed completely wet.

Beyond the frog, like the entrance to a garden, was an archway of bronze vines, with a sign announcing, THE HEART OF THE MATTER.

I stopped to skim the brochure. "Ten related bronzes cast to 1/10 scale," it said. I passed under the arch.

Tommy Loves Rhiann portrayed a crew-cut, sixth-grade Smoke in Levi's and Sneakers holding up a fat frog—with its feet hangingdown like a bunch of flowers—for the inspection of a girl in a sleeveless, scooped-neck dress. The figures were reminiscent of Norman Rockwell, their faces perfectly illustrating Smoke's mischievous glee and sly intelligence, his underlying sadness, Rhiann's feigned disdain.

John's ability to portray emotions was amazing. Which made his inability to express them in person all the more incredible.

Tears leaked from my eyes. I had forgotten to bring tissue and had to run to the ladies' room for paper towels. Equipped, I started in again.

The Monster that Lives in the Dark portrayed Tommy Johnson with photographic reality as he stood, legs splayed, a bottle in one hand and a belt in the other. And *Amy Johnson* was a fierce Madonna defending the child at her feet with a broom and a garbage can lid.

Librarian depicted Mrs. Hammond sharing a book with a teenaged Smoke.

Smoke Loves Rhiann showed seventeen-year-old Smoke, with cigarette dangling from his mouth, pulling the petals off a daisy in the old she-loves-me-she-loves-me-not routine.

In *We All Love Rhiann*, Billy and Steve and Smoke circled a dancing Rhiann with their arms on one another's shoulders as she embraced Billy and looked adoringly at Smoke.

Billy Loves Rhiann was a soldier, with full field kit, M-16, and helmet, hugging a pregnant Rhiann. Her head came just under his chin, her face was buried in his shirt front. Billy's face clearly showed the anguish of parting.

A ghost of the loss I'd felt when Billy left shivered through me like someone walking on my grave.

Mickey Loves Rhiann depicted Mickey bracing his feet as he swung me overhead. His face glowed with good humor and the love he obviously felt.

Mickey and Jimmy showed a smiling Mickey teaching his son to ride his first bike.

John Loves Rhiann was a self-portrait of the artist sculpting the statue of a young Rhiann. The sculptor's expression was adoring, his posture protective.

I had to stop. The story of my relationships with the men I loved was too clearly illustrated.

I hurried outside and walked, sobbing, back to Union Station.

John

After having Rhiann and losing her again, I couldn't bear to see her. Not even at a distance. Not even a glance.

I couldn't bear to not see her, either, but I felt distance was safer, so I didn't go home.

I didn't go to the shop, either. We had nothing urgent scheduled, so I made assignments via phone and told them not to call unless someone died.

I stayed at the studio. Cleaned it. Ordered materials for the work I'd sketched on the wall. Tried to keep busy.

Tried not to think of Rhiann.

Rhiann

The address the shipping company had given me was for a small, single-story brick factory built in a time when factories had large windows and high ceilings, with skylights and wood ceiling beams. The windows along the south side, facing the alley, had been painted over in white and covered by cyclone fencing. The number stenciled on the garage-type door facing east on the narrow lane was duplicated on the regular-sized steel door next to it.

I knocked. Moments later, John opened the door. He was clean and smelled of aftershave, and his hair was wet—he must have just taken a shower. He'd put on loafers but not socks—further proof.

He said, "I thought you'd given up on me."

I put my hand over my heart and fluttered my fingers. "I discovered I still have a frog in my dress."

He stepped aside to let me in. "How did you find me?"

"Your shipper."

"Ah."

I walked to the center of a space too large to call a room, roughly the size of a small gymnasium. It had a clean concrete floor that was chipped and spotted with welding slag. John followed me, hands at his sides. He waited while I looked around. There was an empty easel in the center, beneath the skylight. A tool bench ran along the left side with tools neatly lined up along its length. Others hung on the wall above it, between the windows. In the back corner, an old double-drainboard cast-iron sink sat below a wall-mounted cabinet. Next to the sink stood a wastebasket, and an old refrigerator. Farther along, between doors labeled "Relief" and "Supplies," a cot stood against the wall with a drafting table within easy dropping-from-exhaustion distance. The right side of the room was filled with pallets of cardboard cartons. Nearby were blocks of wood and stone, and a Clark forklift.

The studio was a stark contrast to John's office. Except for abstract charcoal drawings on the walls, there were no pictures or finished works of art. The drawings reminded me of *Guernica.*

"I saw your retrospective."

He looked expectantly. "Well?"

"It was—" As I tried to find the words, I squeezed my lip between my teeth. No tears! "Overwhelming."

He nodded as if he thought that was right. "Guess that's why I didn't send you an invitation."

"Where did you learn to draw?"

"After I got out of Stateville, I got a night job in Chicago. Servicing trucks. It let me have days free. And I had my GED, so I applied at Columbia College. While I was working on my BA, I discovered The School of the Art Institute. They showed me what I was meant to do. It was like discovering swans."

I raised my eyebrows.

"When all your life you've been the ugly duckling."

I touched his arm.

"Don't," he said. "Unless you're willing to go all the way, as we used to put it."

I wrapped my hands around his upper arm and rested my head against his shoulder. "Where have you been all these years?"

He pulled away and pointed to the cot. I sat on it, back to the wall. He leaned his butt against the drafting table and crossed his arms.

"After I left, it was two years before I figured I could run into my old man again without beating him to death."

Remembering the *Monster Who...* sculpture, I shuddered. "He used to beat you. That's where you got the scars."

He nodded.

"Why didn't you ever ask for help?"

"That would've been admitting he'd won."

"That's why in all those years I never saw you without a shirt?"

"I used to duct tape bread bags inside my clothes so I wouldn't bleed through." His voice was curiously flat.

I blinked to stop the tears.

Smoke suddenly materialized in front of me. "No pity!"

He stepped back and became John again. "I want you. Not that."

It occurred to me that I had never seen him cry. I said so.

"I was all cried out by the time I was seven." He said it contemptuously—Smoke again. "I started working out when I was thirteen, when someone put me on to Charles Atlas. When I was fourteen, he came after me with his belt. I grabbed my Louisville slugger and hit a triple against his chest. Broke three ribs. Told him if he ever touched me or my mother again I'd beat him to death. He never came near us after that."

There were a thousand things I wanted to ask: Why did you change your name? And when? Where have you lived all these years? With who?

But it seemed a time for silence, time to reflect on what we'd said already.

There was a long pause.

Finally, I had to ask: "Why didn't you keep in touch?"

"When I came back, you were married. I guess I thought you'd wait for me. I should've asked."

"I couldn't."

He looked puzzled.

"I didn't want our child to be a bastard."

His eyes widened. He pushed away from the drafting table and sat beside me on the cot, not touching. "Did Billy know?"

I nodded.

Billy had had a month's leave before he shipped out. He took me out for ice cream the second night he was back.

After we'd finished, he took my hand and said, "Marry me."

I started to say, "I'm pregnant," but he cut me off.

"Smoke's not coming back," he said. "Your kid needs a father, and I need someone to write to me while I'm gone. When I get back, if you don't love me, I'll give you a divorce."

He'd guessed somehow. I wasn't showing yet; I'd told no one. I didn't answer right away.

He got down on one knee and said, "Rhiann, will you marry me?"

There must've been fifteen people in the Dairy Queen. Most of them stared. Of course I said yes.

Tears spilled over and down my cheeks.

John said, "He was a good man."

I nodded.

"So you had a month together."

"Just two weeks by the time we got the blood tests and license. We went to Chicago, got married at City Hall. We stayed at the Ohio Inn. Then he was gone."

I had a sudden recall of John's retrospective, *Billy Loves Rhiann*. The figure had Billy's face, but Smoke's expression the morning he'd taken leave of me three times.

I said, "Why did you move next door?"

"Do I have to spell it out?"

"Yes. Please."

"When I heard about Mickey's death, I wanted to be sure you were safe. And I hoped...I thought maybe I'd catch your eye."

"Why didn't you identify yourself?" We both knew what

I meant by that.

"I wanted you to know the man I've become."

He didn't add, "And love him," but it was in his eyes. He said, "Where do we go from here?"

"Maybe we could start over—I'm Rhiann Fahey. I'm still reeling from the death of my husband. But I'll get over it one day."

He wiped his hand on his jeans, then shoved it at me. "I'm John, your new neighbor, and I'd like to know you better. When you're ready."

"Deal," I said as I shook. I felt the sexual charge arc between us like slow lightning.

He must have felt it, too, because he let go of my hand as if it were scalding. He said, "Now that that's settled, let's go get something to eat."

Old habits. Our standard response—whenever things were tense or we were bored or too exhausted to think of what to do next—was to hit McDonald's or Denny's and sit around sharing French fries and swapping insults.

He got up and pulled me to my feet. "There's a decent mom-and-pop café about a mile from here. I usually walk, but you have to pick up Jimmy soon, so maybe we should drive."

I looked at my watch. "My parking meter's about to expire, so we might as well take my car."

"Okay." He walked over to the sink and took his wallet and keys out of the cabinet above it.

We were out in the alley, and he was locking the door when his phone rang. He said, "Damn. I'd better get that."

"I'll get the car and come back."

I'd parked three blocks away because I wasn't sure of the studio's location. When I got back to the car, I had five minutes left on the meter. From habit, I looked for a parking enforcer, noticed a meter maid. She was looking from an expired meter to the sheriff's police car parked next to it.

We were inside the town limits. Sheriff's police didn't often have business there. I went close enough to see the unit number painted on the trunk: 96. Rory's car.

"Call the police." I told the meter maid. I shoved the paper with the address at her before I took off running.

John

The phone call was from my garage manager, who wanted to know if you really had to take the valve covers off a boss '71 Mustang to change the plugs. It took a couple minutes to convince him it wasn't a joke—just one of Ford's "better ideas," and to tell him the most efficient way to deal with it. We were nearly finished when I heard the door open. Rhiann must be back. I put my hand over the mouthpiece and called out, "Be right there." Then I said good-bye, and hung up.

I turned around just as Deputy Sheriff Sinter came in with his gun drawn. "Put your hands up," he said. He was in uniform, wearing state trooper shades and black leather gloves. The gun was a nine-millimeter semiautomatic. While I complied, he reached behind him to push in the lock button on the door handle.

He came toward me and his attention seemed divided between keeping an eye on me and checking the place out. "Who else is here?" he demanded.

"No one." I wondered what he was doing outside his

jurisdiction. Then he came closer, and I could smell the booze. Whatever he had in mind was personal, and I suspected that he'd waited till Rhiann left so she wouldn't interfere.

He said, "Get over against the wall." He pointed to a stretch that was bare of everything but sketches.

Every cell in my body screamed, "No!" but he wasn't drunk enough to miss at that range. I turned around and fear snaked up my spine. When I got about three feet from the wall, he slammed the gun against the right side of my face. I stumbled and threw my hands up to break my fall. He put a hand against my back and shoved. "Assume the position." Then he let me have it in the right kidney with his fist.

I smashed headfirst into the wall. I turned my head in time to save my nose but left a smear of blood where my cheek and jaw hit. My hands blurred the sketches.

Pressing the barrel of his gun into the hollow at the base of my skull, Sinter battered the insides of my ankles with his foot. "Spread 'em." I was already close to doing splits. "Don't move a muscle."

I felt the old helplessness roll over me. Guards at Stateville had impressed me with their power using such threats, following through with beatings that left me groggy and swollen. Sinter held the gun in place while he changed hands on the grip, then fumbled at his belt for his handcuffs. Despair almost made me lie down and quit as he snapped them on my right wrist.

"Bring your hand around behind your back—real slow."

I did what I was told.

"Good. Now the other one."

He kept tension on my right wrist and the gun against my skull until my left hand was behind me. The gun stayed in place until he'd fumbled the second cuff on and snugged it tight. Then he stepped back and said, "Turn around." As I did, he holstered his weapon, then buried his fist in my gut.

I saw it coming and tensed, but it doubled me over and left me close to puking.

Sinter said, "You really shouldn't resist."

I said nothing.

He slid a half pint of Early Times from his back pocket and unscrewed the cap. He took a long pull, then replaced the cap and the flask. It seemed to put him in a better mood.

"How long you been bonkin' her?"

I shook my head, more to clear it than deny the charge. "We're just neighbors."

"Yeah, right. That's why you got a couple hundred pictures of her on your walls."

I didn't answer.

"You got beaver shots upstairs in your boudoir?" He pronounced it "bood-war."

The studio seemed to shrink and elongate until it was only me and him with a dark tunnel of hatred between us. I felt cold with rage. It must've showed because he laughed and hit me again.

I've got to fight back, I thought, or he'll beat me to death. But I couldn't seem to get my breath, and my legs didn't work right. I tried to distract him: "You learn big words like 'boudoir' in cop school?" There was no response. "You even know what it means?"

He aimed a kick at my crotch. I rolled sideways, and it caught my thigh—Painful but survivable.

He was moving in to finish me when the overhead garage door started to creak upward.

Rhiann!

Sinter stopped and reversed, then drew his gun and started toward the door.

Quietly as I could, I pushed off from the wall and wobbled after him. When the door got halfway up, I could see Rhiann holding the garage door opener I keep in my Jeep. Sinter pointed the gun at her. I aimed for the hollow behind his knee and let him have it with all I had. His leg flew out from under him. He threw his arm out. The gun went off as he hit the floor. No telling where the bullet went.

Momentum carried me past him, and I caught a glimpse of Rhiann. She looked terrified but unhurt.

I pivoted and aimed a kick at Sinter's gun hand. It connected squarely. The gun discharged again. There was a crackle of breaking glass, and the gun flew across the studio. It landed with a metallic clatter before skittering under the workbench.

I was aiming my third kick—at Sinter's head—when Rhiann's voice cut through the fog of pain and rage.

"SMOKE, NO!"

Rhiann

My scream threw John off balance—with his hands cuffed behind him, he couldn't put his arms out. I dropped the garage door opener and ran, grabbed him just in time to stop his fall. He braced himself against me, swaying like a drunk. He was bruised and bloody but I threw my arms around him and pressed my face against his chest.

I heard a siren, then the approaching car, and an Alva police cruiser pulled up next to the Jeep. The cop who got out looked to be in his thirties. The way he moved as he came toward us said he'd been around long enough to be savvy and cynical.

At that point, John's knees buckled and he would have fallen if I hadn't been holding him. But he was too heavy; he would have hit hard if the Alva cop hadn't jumped forward and caught him. He sat John down on the floor and said, "What's going on?"

Rory started to uncoil from his fetal position. I let go of John and leaned toward Rory, nearly gagging at the smell of alcohol.

"Rory," I said. "If you move a hair, I'll kick you to death myself."

He froze. Then he relaxed and told the cop, "I came here to arrest this guy. And he jumped me."

John didn't say anything, but I couldn't keep quiet. "That's not true! He followed me here and beat John. And he tried to shoot me!"

"He was resisting arrest. I had to use force."

"Liar," I said. I looked at the cop. "He's drunk!"

The disgusted look on the cop's face made me think he agreed. "Where's your service gun?" he asked Rory.

"They have it."

"No!" I said. "John kicked it out of his hand." I pointed. "It slid under the bench."

The cop walked over and retrieved the gun. He ejected the magazine and pocketed it, then checked the chamber. He walked outside and put the gun on the hood of his car.

While he called in on his radio, I dug my key ring from

my pocket and used Mickey's handcuff key to let John out of the cuffs. I slid them across the floor, toward the door. John pulled his legs up and rested his forearms on his knees, showing off bruised, skinned wrists.

When the cop came back, he picked up the handcuffs without comment, then walked over to where Rory was gingerly checking the damage to his hand. "What'd this guy do?" the Alva cop asked him.

Rory hesitated a bit too long before he said, "Unlawful possession of a firearm."

"Yeah?" the cop said. I could see he'd noticed the delay, too. "Where is it?"

"In my pocket."

There must have been a gun—Rory wouldn't have told a lie so easily caught out—but I knew it wasn't John's.

I said, "That's Rory's drop gun."

Rory looked at him and said, "She's fucking him. She'd say anything to get him off."

If he'd been close enough, I'd've slapped him, and it must've showed on my face.

"How do you know about drop guns?" the cop asked me.

"My husband was a cop. Mickey Fahey."

The Alva cop raised his eyebrows. He pointed to John. "Who's he?"

"A friend. We went to school together."

The cop turned back to Rory. "Where *is* this gun?"

"I told you, in my pocket."

"Okay. Put your hands over your head and roll over on your face."

"I can't. I got a smashed knee and some broken ribs."

"Roll over or I'll break some more."

"You gonna believe a convicted felon and his whore over a fellow cop?" Rory demanded.

"He hasn't said anything," the cop said, "but what I see fits her story better than yours." He cuffed Rory's hands behind him with his own handcuffs, and started going through his pockets, laying out the drop gun, a hip flask, and assorted keys and pocket junk in a row next to Rory's knees.

"So I'm gonna keep an eye on all of you, let my sergeant sort this out."

John

The sergeant turned out to be someone I knew. He listened to the Alva patrolman's version of things, and took Rhiann out to his car to get her side. Then he came back in the studio and talked to me.

While he was interviewing Rory—now handcuffed in the back of the Alva squad car—Rhiann came inside to put ice on my face.

The sergeant came back in. "I'm taking Deputy Sinter to the lockup. You folks'll have to come to the station and sign a complaint if you want me to hold him."

Rhiann said, "If we do, will you take away his guns?"

"Yes, ma'am. And if he's convicted, he won't get 'em back."

Rhiann

We never did get lunch. John drove us to the cop shop in my car, and we spent a good hour waiting in the lobby while they did the paperwork.

Someone must've called Sheriff Linden, because he came into the station like a summer storm. He glared at John and me. He didn't take his hat off as he stalked up to the counter and asked to see the chief. After a few minutes, he was led into the back.

The sergeant came out and brought us coffee in mugs that said PROPERTY OF THE COUNTY JAIL.

When the sheriff came back to the lobby, he looked like he was ready to kill. But he walked over to me and removed his hat.

"I owe you an apology, Mrs. Fahey. I was wrong about Rory." He looked at John. "'Bout you, too, Devlin." He put his hat on. "Rory won't bother you again."

By the time the sheriff was halfway to the door, John was shaking.

"What's the matter, John?" I asked.

"Nothing." His shaking turned into hearty laughter. "It's just like old times."

"What?"

"Even if we didn't start it, here we are again, in the principal's office."

When the sergeant came out with our paperwork, we were still laughing like a couple of silly teens.

Jimmy

I about freaked when Ma came to take me home from the hospital. Her clothes were covered with blood.

"I'm sorry we're late, sweetheart."

Sweetheart? She hadn't called me that since I was ten.

And *we*? I looked toward the door and spotted John. His clothes were clean, but his face looked like someone slammed it against the side of a bridge.

And there was something else about him—he couldn't take his eyes off my mother. I mean—even more than usual.

I looked back at Ma. "Are you okay?"

She smiled. "Fine." She noticed I was staring at her dress. "I didn't have time to change."

"What happened? You're scaring me."

"We had an encounter with Deputy Sinter," John said.

"Holy shit! What's *he* look like?"

Mom giggled. "He's in jail."

I pointed to her dress. "Is that *his* blood?"

"No. John's. If Rory'd gotten close enough to get his blood on me, he'd be dead."

"We can talk about it in the car," John said. "Let's get out of here before they charge you for another day."

With my crutches, it took me a long time to get to the living room. It was the last Friday in October; I'd been home from the hospital just one day. Before I opened the door, I looked out the front window. Stephanie's car was in the drive. No driver. I almost fell over trying to get the door open fast.

Beth was on the porch, her face all red and puffy. It took me a whole ten seconds to figure out she'd been crying.

"Beth, what's wrong?" I grabbed her hand and pulled her into the house and hugged her.

She pulled away, and I had to hop around on my good leg to keep from falling on my ass. "C'mon," I said. I got my crutches under control and gimped off toward the family room.

Beth followed. "Is your mom home?"

"At work."

We got into the kitchen; I asked if she wanted anything to drink. She shook her head.

"Okay," I said. "Sit down and tell me what's the matter."

I propped my butt against the counter and leaned my crutches on it. I pointed to the couch. Beth threw herself onto it and folded her arms across her chest. She was so small and limber she could almost touch her fingers together behind her back. She bit her lip.

"Beth, what's wrong?"

She looked up at me, then looked away. "I missed my period."

"So?" I can be pretty dim sometimes.

"I've never been late before. I'm pregnant."

"Couldn't there be another reason?"

"No. I took one of those do-it-yourself tests. I'm pregnant."

I suddenly felt like I'd been run over by a truck. I grabbed my crutches and hobbled over to sit next to her. I didn't touch her.

"How long before you have to tell anyone?"

She looked at me like I was crazy. "This isn't just gonna go away. In another couple months everybody'll know just by looking at me."

"No. I know. But that gives us time to figure out what to do."

"Us?"

"I got you into this."

She stared at me for a very long time, looking mad. Then she giggled.

We both started laughing.

"It's not funny," she said.

That made us stop. For about seven-tenths of a second. We looked at each other and started laughing again. Hysterically. Until we had tears in our eyes.

Then Beth started sobbing.

I grabbed her and held her. She put her face against me and just cried. I braced my good leg and pulled her onto my lap. I held her until she stopped sobbing and was asleep.

I must have drifted off, too.

My ma woke me turning on the kitchen light. She had a bag of groceries that she put on the counter.

It was dark outside. Beth was still sleeping on my lap. She looked like a little girl. My girl. She looked too young to be a mother. Or a wife. But it was too late to worry about that.

When I said, "Hi, Ma," Beth opened her eyes.

Ma was cool. She said, "Hi, Beth," like it was completely normal to come home and find her sleeping on my lap on the family room couch.

Beth said, "Hi, Mrs. Fahey." She looked out the window. It was already dark. "Oh, my God. What time is it?"

"Almost six," Ma said.

"I'm gonna get killed." Beth stood up. "I was s'posed to be back with the car by now."

"Why don't you call home, explain that you were delayed. And ask if you can stay for dinner."

"No. Thank you. It's not my—It's my friend Stephanie's car."

"Beth," I said, reaching for her hand. "Chill. Call Steph and tell her what happened. Ask her what she wants you to do."

Beth said, "Where's—"

"The phone's over there." I pointed to the wall phone by the outside door.

"Better yet," Ma said, "why don't you use the phone in the living room?"

"Good idea," I said.

Beth said, "Thank you," and went toward the living room door.

I mouthed, "Thanks, Ma," behind Beth's back.

Ma started putting the groceries away. "John's coming for dinner." She tried to sound casual, but there was something in her voice I hadn't heard since she used to kid with my dad about "getting lucky."

"That's cool." It *was* cool if she was starting to notice John.

When Beth came back, she looked better. "Steph said she's got me covered." She looked at Ma. "I'd be happy to stay for dinner. Can I help with anything?"

• • •

Beth and John hit it off right away. Another good sign. I wondered if I could ask him what to do about the mess we were in. Tomorrow.

As it got later, Beth got more and more nervous. Even John noticed.

He asked her, “Is something wrong?”

“It’s just—I’ve never driven home alone this late at night before.”

Ma said, “Maybe you should stay overnight and drive home in the morning. You don’t have school.”

“Oh, no. Thanks. But if my folks ever found out, they’d kill me. And you, too.”

John said, “How ’bout I follow you in my car?”

“I couldn’t ask you to do that.”

“You didn’t. I offered.”

Beth nodded.

“Or if it’s okay with his mother, Jimmy could ride with you and I’ll bring him back.” He looked at Ma.

She seemed surprised, but she nodded.

So that’s how it went down. Except Ma rode along, too. In John’s car.

John

It didn’t surprise me to see the state investigator again. Not long after Jimmy came home from the hospital, Crowley came into the shop; Davey pointed him to my office. I’d just made coffee. I offered Crowley a cup, and we sat in the office to drink it.

"What can I do for you today, Sergeant?"

"Tell me about your little run-in with Deputy Sheriff Sinter."

"He's got a jones for Rhiann Fahey and apparently sees me as a rival. He's tried to beat me to death on two occasions."

"That's a pretty serious charge."

"Did you read the Alva police report?"

He nodded. "I wasn't taking your complaint about him stalking Mrs. Fahey too seriously until he backed you up with that little rampage." Crowley shook his head. "Lucky for us he's criminally stupid. Turns out, he *is* the cop those football players mentioned. The sheriff gave me a copy of the ticket he wrote them."

"So he thought about what they said about being set up and figured out that Jimmy used him. And he decided to get payback."

Crowley nodded. "Looks that way. Proving it won't be easy."

"He had plenty of opportunities to get at Jimmy's car—always doing radar on our street. Jimmy always parked in the driveway."

"I'd like to get a little more before we bring him in for questioning. Meanwhile, we're revisiting several previous assault complaints."

"Good. Has he been suspended?"

"Reassigned to clerical duties pending disposition of the charges. The sheriff's holding his gun—the one he admits to possessing."

"I suspect it's not the only one he owns."

Crowley finished his coffee and put the mug on my desk. "We're looking into that, too."

Jimmy

"They want two hundred and fifty for it," John said. "Not a bad deal. And it's an automatic, so you can drive it with your cast."

That was the clincher. No way I could manage a clutch with my bum leg. And I could always trade the car once I was out of the cast.

"Deal," I said. "I'll get Finn to drive me to the bank. Tell them I'll pick it up tomorrow."

"If you like, I can advance you the money. You could drive it home today."

"Thanks, John."

When I showed up for work Friday afternoon, Dr. Pulaski wasn't glad to see me. The back door was locked, so I had to go in the front. The waiting room was jammed—everybody trying to get their pets in to see the doc before the weekend. The receptionist told me to go in one of the exam rooms and wait for the doctor—which was weird. It took about ten minutes before he came in.

"Beth's not here," he said right away. No "Hi, Jimmy. How are you?" No "Glad to have you back."

"Did something happen?"

"Yeah, something happened. Her father showed up here with his shorts in a bunch because he found out you two were sneaking around behind his back. He blames me for not telling him. So she's gone. The best kennel girl I ever had. You're gone, too. You're trouble." He turned and walked out, just like that.

I wasn't sure what to do next. Or where to find Beth. It sounded like she was grounded for life, so she'd probably be at home. But if I just drove up and rang the bell, her father would probably beat me to death. Then I remembered I had her number.

I drove to a gas station and used the pay phone. After five rings, a woman's voice said, "You've reached the Wilding residence. We're not able to come to the phone right now..." I hung up. Fast.

Wilding residence? I hadn't dialed my grandmother's number by mistake. And the voice on the answering machine didn't sound like Rosa. Maybe Finn wrote down the number wrong. Or maybe it was some kind of joke. I asked the gas station guy for a telephone book and looked up Wilding. There were two listed in Greenville—my grandparents and a Robert Wilding. Which had to be my uncle Bobby. I checked the address. Beth's address. That wasn't possible. But when I read it again, it hadn't changed.

I started to feel sick. But my cousin's name was Liz.

And Steve told me she was mean and ugly. And Steve was probably putting me on.

Liz? Beth? Elizabeth?

It was too gross! It was like Oedipus. It was too late to do anything about it.

I wondered if Beth had figured it out.

I'll bet her dad did. He was probably mad enough to lynch me. Or set me on fire. He was probably mad enough to scare Dr. Pulaski to death, even if he didn't tell him the whole story.

I had to talk to Beth about it. Had to see her. But how, without risking both our lives?

As I hobbled back to the car, I got an idea. Nobody in Greenville had seen my new car. Nobody would recognize it. I could just drive to Beth's house and park nearby and wait. If I stayed out of sight until dark, I might get a chance to see her.

Which is pretty much how it went down. I drove to the megamall on the interstate and used most of my cash to get supplies—a pair of kid's binoculars from Toys "R" Us, then a six-pack of Coke, a big bag of Cheetos, paper towels, duct tape, flashlight, and batteries from Kmart. And a cane, so I could ditch my crutches. I was ready for anything.

Except figuring out what to do about the mess I was in.

When I got to Beth's neighborhood, I parked and studied the houses. It was close to Halloween and almost everyone had put up decorations—pumpkins, scarecrows, fake spiderwebs. Beth's house had paper cutouts of witches and ghosts stuck on the windows. There was a light blue Cadillac DeVille parked out front.

Fortunately, it was getting dark pretty early. So by the time I'd gotten bored with the scenery, it was dark enough to recon.

I didn't have to. As soon as it was dark, Beth's front porch lights went on. A woman and two kids came out and got into the Caddy. The woman started the engine and climbed over into the passenger's seat. And waited. For about ten minutes.

Then a big man came out and paused on the porch to talk to someone still inside. I studied him through my binoculars. It was my uncle Bob, all right.

I was glad I hadn't eaten; I felt sick.

"I don't want to hear another word," Bob yelled in through the door. "Just stay in your room!"

He had to be yelling at Beth!

The thought of her made me feel better. If they were going out, I'd have a chance to see her.

Bob slammed the door. He stalked to the Cadillac and climbed in, then slammed the door. He burned rubber as he backed out of the drive, even more as he took off down the street.

Just in case he forgot something and had to come back, I gave him five whole minutes before I got out of the car.

Beth didn't answer the door. I rang the bell until I got tired of hearing it. I tried knocking. Finally, I hobbled around the house yelling her name as loud as I could. She was standing on the porch when I got back around to the front. She had on a bathrobe and looked like she'd been crying.

"Jimmy, get out of here."

"I'm not leaving until I talk to you."

"Are you crazy? If my dad finds you here, he'll kill you!"

It hit me—I didn't care. I couldn't imagine life without Beth. I shrugged.

She took me by the shoulders and shook me. "I am not exaggerating. My dad will kill you."

I crossed my arms and stood my ground.

She looked around. There was no sign of the Cadillac,

but a neighbor across the street was standing in his doorway, staring. Beth grabbed my arm and pulled me inside.

She closed the door and leaned back against it. Her eyes filled with tears. "What are we gonna do?"

"Your dad knows that you're pregnant?"

She nodded and started sobbing. "He says you're my cousin. He wants me to get an abortion."

"What do you say?"

"Are you?"

I nodded. "Billy Wilding was my birth father." I moved closer and put my arms around her. And stroked her hair.

She pushed me away. "Did you know?"

"Not till today."

She balled up her hands and pounded my chest. Not hard. In frustration. "What are we gonna do?"

"What do you want to do?"

"Honestly?"

"Yeah." I knew I sounded annoyed but we were wasting time.

"I don't want an abortion."

"So don't get one."

"You don't understand. My dad—"

"Is an asshole. But it's your body. Your kid." My kid!

"He's not giving me a choice. He's taking me on Monday."

"The hell he is. Get some stuff together. Let's get out of here."

"But where can we go? He'll call the police."

I took her face in my hands. "Look. I don't care if we *are* cousins. I love you. I don't want your dad to hurt you. Or me. But he's just a grown-up goon. A bully. You can't give in to a bully."

She was real quiet for a minute.

I tried one more argument. "Beth, if you don't want me to ever touch you again, it's okay. Or if you never want to see me again. And if you don't care about getting an abortion, I can live with that. But don't stay here and go through with it just because of your old man. You'll hate yourself if you do."

"Would you hate me?"

I shook my head. "I could never hate you."

She studied my face for a long time. Then she said, "I'll go get dressed."

I had to stop at Steve's to get my stuff. I figured he'd be working, and planned to leave a note, but as soon as I put my key in the lock the door opened.

"Hey, Jimmy. You're in early." He looked behind me and spotted Beth. "Liz, nice to see you. You two finally got introduced."

Beth blushed, then started laughing. Hysterically.

I said, "Can we come in?"

Steve swung the door open and stepped back. "My casa is your casa."

I put my arm around Beth and guided her inside. We followed Steve into the living room.

Steve looked at my cast and said, "Almost good as new, huh?"

"It's mending."

"Well, sit down. Make yourselves at home."

Beth said, "Thanks, but we really can't stay."

"Just came by for a pit stop?"

I said, "Actually, I came to get my stuff."

Steve gave me a suspicious look and waited. Then he crossed his arms and said, "One of you is going to tell me what's going on."

So we did.

When we finished, he just sighed and said, "All this because your dickhead father—" He looked at Beth. "Judges everyone by himself."

"What do you mean?"

Steve looked at her and grinned. "He and Rachel had to get married because you were on the way. I guess he thought if he kept you away from boys, history couldn't repeat itself." He shook his head. "What are you gonna do?"

"Go somewhere her father can't find us until we figure out what we're gonna do."

"Not much of a plan."

Before I could answer, a phone rang.

"Steve, you got a phone!"

"Yeah," he said as he got up to answer. "I thought it might be nice to talk to your mother once in a while."

When he came back, he told me, "That was your aunt Rachel. Bob's on his way over, loaded for bear. You better hit the road."

"He's coming here?"

"That's what she said."

"He'll kill you, even if he doesn't find us here."

"Don't worry. As soon as you two are gone, I'm callin' the cavalry."

Rhiann

Friday afternoon, John insisted he service my car, after which he took me to dinner while Davey washed and detailed it. By the time we were finished eating—and talking—it was nearly ten o'clock.

"Let's leave your car at the shop tonight," John said. "We can pick it up tomorrow after breakfast."

"But what'll I do tonight?"

"If you come home with me, you can look at my etchings."

Which is just what I did.

Jimmy

Early the next morning, I stopped at Finn's—to get him before he left for work. "Wait in the car," I told Beth. "I'll just be a minute."

Finn's ma let me in. "Good morning, Jimmy. Finn's in the kitchen."

He yawned when he saw me. "You're up early. Hey, how come you're not in Greenville?"

"I got canned."

"That why you're so bummed?"

"No. Listen, I need you to front me some cash."

"Sure. How much?"

"As much as you got."

"Why?"

"Better you don't know."

"You rob a bank or somethin'? No, wait. Then you wouldn't need money. What's this about?" He got that you'd-better-give look on his face and waited.

"Beth's pregnant, and we gotta get out of town."

"Why run away? Where would you go?"

"Maybe we'll go to Vegas and get married. Beth's dad is trying to make her get an abortion."

"What about your mom?"

"Better she doesn't know where we went. Then she doesn't have to lie."

Finn shook his head sadly. "You're off your fuckin' nut."

"Are you gonna lend me the money?"

He shrugged. "Yeah. Wait here while I get it."

He was back in two minutes. He handed me a roll of bills and waited while I stashed it in my pocket, then he held out his hand. "Good luck, man. You're gonna need it."

"Thanks." I started to go, then had a thought. "Finn, what happens when you marry your first cousin?"

"You turn into a hillbilly."

"What?"

"My *dad* says half the hillbillies in the country're married to their first cousins."

"I'm serious, man."

"Seriously, you can't marry your first cousin. It's against the law."

"What if you didn't tell?"

There was a long wait while he thought about it. Then he said, "Probably nothin' if no one found out."

"No shit?"

"Remember when Hutchings's dogs had puppies?"

"The yellow Labs?"

He nodded. "The father dog was the bitch's brother. And none of 'em came out with two heads."

"Yeah, but those are dogs. I'm talking about people."

"A lot of people are dogs."

"Don't be a dickhead!"

"Biology's biology, man. If you married your cousin—if you *could* marry your cousin—you'd probably get kicked out of your church, and everybody'd think you were a retard.

"But that wouldn't matter to your genes."

After we left Finn's, we went to my house to get some things. I figured it was safe. Ma wasn't home—her car wasn't in the drive. I told Beth to raid the fridge and pack us a lunch, and I went up to get my emergency stash. While I was at it, I threw some clean stuff in my duffel and dug out my junior class ring. It wasn't a diamond, but I guessed it would do until I could get one.

I nearly ran into my ma when I came back in the kitchen. I couldn't tell who looked more shocked—her or Beth. It was one of those "Oh, shit" moments.

Then Ma and Beth started to talk at once. Then they both shut up.

Ma recovered first. "Good morning, Beth. Jimmy."

I said, "Morning, Ma," and Beth said, "Good morning, Mrs. Fahey," at the same time.

"Where's your car, Ma?"

"I left it at John's shop for service."

Before I could ask her where she'd been, or how she got

home, she said, “Don’t you two have work today?”

Beth got really red. And I must have, too, because Ma suddenly went on alert. “What’s the matter with you?”

Beth and I looked at each other—we couldn’t help it. Ma went to full parental vigilance mode. She pointed at the couch and said, “Sit.”

We did.

Ma looked from Beth’s lunch bag to my duffel and said, “Going somewhere?”

Which caused Beth to break out in a crying fit. So, of course, we had to tell her.

Even though I didn’t want to run crying to my ma to bail us out, it felt kinda good getting it off my chest.

Ma didn’t freak. She handed Beth a box of Kleenex and asked, “What did you think you were going to do?”

“Go somewhere my dad can’t find us.”

“You didn’t think he would look here?”

“We weren’t gonna stay,” I said. “Just get some stuff and leave.”

“Where?”

I shrugged.

Ma said, “You’re *not* running away.”

“But my dad’ll kill Jimmy!”

“And make Beth get an abortion.”

That’s when the phone rang.

Ma gave us a schoolteacher look and said, “Don’t move,” then went to answer the phone. When she said, “Steve?” I limped into the living room to listen on the extension.

“Bob’s on the way,” Steve said. “He jumped me and knocked me down the basement stairs. I didn’t tell him where you live, but you’re in the book. You better call the cops.”

Ma said, "Thanks, Steve," and hung up. She sounded really calm.

Before she could dial 911 or anything, we heard pounding on the front door.

I looked out and saw the blue DeVille. "Ma, call the cops!"

She called back, "Who's there?"

"Beth's dad."

"Call the police," I heard her tell Beth as she came charging from the kitchen.

The pounding on the door stopped. Something started crashing against it.

I looked out again and saw Uncle Bobby whaling on the door with a baseball bat.

It took him about thirty seconds to break the bat. He tossed the pieces aside and started smashing the door with his foot.

The doorframe shattered like a movie prop. The door flew open.

And Uncle Bobby—Beth's dad—came through the doorway like the Terminator.

Rhiann

Bob came through the door like a pro tackle. He was two inches taller than my son and at least a hundred pounds heavier. He crossed the living room in four strides and slammed Jimmy against the wall, sending his cane flying. I threw myself at them. Bob swatted me aside, then hit Jimmy in the face.

John charged in as the blow landed. Jimmy slid to the floor. Before Bob could touch him again, John smashed the bully facefirst into the wall. He grabbed Bob's collar and dragged him back against the side of Mickey's old recliner and threw him on it. Bob didn't get up.

I went to Jimmy, who pushed me away when I tried to feel for damage. "I'm all right," he muttered. He didn't have the same response to Beth when she came running from the kitchen. She slipped past her father, her eyes wide.

Bob didn't notice. It had been nearly twenty years since anyone stood up to him, much less knocked him silly. He seemed to be in shock.

I got to my feet. As I stepped around the recliner to confront him, John got out of my way. But he stayed close.

I got in Bob's face. "Can you give me one reason why I shouldn't have you arrested?"

"Incest," he managed to gasp. "That bastard of yours got my daughter pregnant. His cousin!" He opened and closed his mouth several times, but no more sound came out.

"Jimmy's not Beth's *blood* cousin," I said. "Billy wasn't his biological father."

"You can't get him off by lying."

"It's easy enough to prove. What was your brother's blood type?"

"B positive."

"Well, mine is O negative. And Jimmy's is A negative. Do you remember enough biology to know what that means?"

I could tell by the surprised, relieved looks on their faces that Beth and Jimmy did.

Bob took a minute to consider, then said, "You sleep

around a lot?"

Behind me, I could *feel* John clenching his fists. I backed into him and reached behind me for his hand. He gave it.

"You tricked my brother into marrying you," Bob insisted. "You told him it was his kid, didn't you?"

"Billy asked me to marry him because he loved me. We got married when we did because he didn't want our kid to be called a bastard."

"You just said he wasn't Billy's."

"Not biologically. But legally, he's Billy's child. Billy would have been his father if he'd lived."

"Whoever his father was, I'm gonna see the kid goes to jail for rape. She was only sixteen!"

"Daddy, no!"

He looked over his shoulder.

Beth was sitting on her feet, twisting Jimmy's class ring round and round on her left thumb. Jimmy was still sitting against the wall, but he had one arm protectively around her.

It seemed to take Bob a long time to realize who was there, to understand what she was saying. Finally he said, "Shut up, Liz!"

"If you send him to jail, I'll just marry him when he gets out!"

Up to this point, John had been silent, hanging back, letting us deal with Bob. Now he held up a hand to silence Beth, keeping his eyes on her father. He disengaged his hand from my grip and gently set me to one side so he faced Bob directly.

"Still picking on the young and the female, Bobby boy? You haven't changed much."

"Who the hell are you?"

"A close friend of the family. A friend of your brother's, too. And I happen to know everything Rhiann said is true."

Bob sat for a moment with his mouth open, then said, "I know you. Who *are* you?"

"They used to call me Smoke."

I could tell from the amazed expression on my son's face that he'd heard some of the legends.

John ignored everyone but Bob. "Unless you're ready to sell everything you own to pay your legal fees, you're going to back off and accept whatever decision Beth and Jimmy make."

Bob's eyes widened and he paled.

He'd been a senior when I was sixteen, a linebacker on the football team. Shortly after the start of football season, he noticed me, and asked me out. I told him I wasn't interested, but he persisted.

One day he started to get grabby. Billy came to my rescue and got knocked around for his trouble. Neither of us mentioned the incident. Smoke would've paid Bobby back with interest and gotten himself expelled. But Billy couldn't hide his fat ear or split lip, and I had a mean bruise above my elbow. Smoke eventually made us give it up.

The day after he found out he told us to meet him at the football field. We both knew there'd be trouble—the team practiced right after school. We showed up because Smoke told us to and we were used to doing what he said. But we were nervous.

Billy and I waited behind the farthest goalpost. Smoke

took a position between us, a few feet back. He looked tough in his 501 jeans and motorcycle boots. His navy T-shirt was a size too small and showed off the muscles he'd been building.

"Smoke, what are we doing?" Billy asked.

"Role-playing. Think of me as D'Artagnan. And you're Athos; Steve's Aramis." Smoke pulled out an imaginary sword and whipped the air with it, then put it away.

"Does that make me Porthos?" I asked.

"No! You're one of my many admirers of the female persuasion."

Not far from the truth, though I didn't say so.

It took fifteen minutes for the players to get tired or the coach curious. He said something, and Bobby came downfield at a hurried walk. He looked from Billy to me and back. "What're you doing here?"

Smoke stepped forward. "They're with me."

"Yeah? Who're you?"

Smoke just smiled. "You know what they call guys who pick on smaller guys and girls?"

"What?"

"Bullies. Are you a bully, Bobby boy?"

"You got some nerve," Bobby said. "You come here three against one—no!—two and a dyke against one—"

"ONE?" Smoke interrupted. "I count sixteen of you. Seventeen with Coach."

The coach had gotten tired of waiting and was heading our way.

Bobby didn't notice. He half yelled, "You're a fuckin' nutcase!"

Smoke gave him a demonic grin.

"What do you *want*?" Bobby demanded.

"I want you to leave my friends alone. I mean, just because you're Billy's older brother doesn't give you the right to whale on him. YOU'RE NOT HIS FATHER!"

Bobby shook his head as if Smoke were hopeless. He pointed at me. "I suppose she's your girlfriend."

"My girl. My friend. My little sister." He took off an imaginary hat and bowed to me—D'Artagnan saluting his queen. "My Frog Princess."

I giggled.

Smoke turned to Bobby. "She's nothing to you except off limits. You understand?"

"If I don't, what're you gonna do about it?"

"You don't want to know."

At that point, the coach reached our position. "What's going on?"

Smoke turned to him. "I had a burning football question I thought Bobby boy might be able to answer."

The coach fell for it. "What's that?"

Smoke turned back and answered Bobby's previous question with one of his own: "How much pain can a linebacker stand before he goes blubbering home to mommy?"

"Are you threatening one of my players?" Coach demanded.

Smoke looked at him. "In front of the whole football team and the coach? I'd have to be—" He whirled to face Bobby. *"Crazy!"*

Bobby took a step back. Obviously, he thought Smoke *was* crazy.

Coach said. "Who *are* you?"

"A talent scout for the Bears."

"Your *name*," Coach said.

"Smoke. As in, 'Where there's fire, there's smoke.'"

"I've heard of you." Coach looked uncomfortable. "You're trouble. Get the hell out of here."

Smoke made another exaggerated bow. "As you wish." He turned to Bob. "See you around, Bobby." He put his arms around Billy's neck and mine and steered us away from the field.

As we left, we heard the coach tell Bobby, "You keep away from those losers."

John

I let Rhiann decide Bob Wilding's fate. She opted for making peace. And for compromise. She said an ex-football player attacking a cripple was probably felony battery and offered to forget about pressing charges if Bob would lay off the kids. She told him his statutory rape case wouldn't hold up with the two minors so close in age. I don't know if she was bluffing, but Bob believed her. The arrival of the sheriff's new deputy seemed anticlimactic, but reinforced her position.

They managed to convince the cop that Beth's call was a false alarm, a family dispute that had gotten out of hand. Jimmy claimed his new bruises were from his accident, and Bob was his favorite father-in-law-to-be.

Before he took his daughter and went home, I told him she'd better be in school Monday morning, unharmed, or every child welfare agency in the state would be at his door.

Bob didn't say a word when Jimmy kissed Beth goodbye and told her he would call her later.

After they drove away, Rhiann announced she was making dinner and ordered me to stay. Then she went inside and left me and Jimmy to work things out.

"Are all families this screwed up?" Jimmy asked.

"Probably. But most people tend to think theirs is the norm, so they don't think of their family as odd."

"Are you really Smoke?"

"I was. Long ago."

"Steve said you loved my mother."

"I do. She's always made me want to be better."

"That's the way Beth makes me feel."

He was quiet for a long time; I let the silence draw him out. "If Billy wasn't—" Jimmy reddened. "Who?"

"Who's your biological father?"

"Yeah."

"It seems I am."

"All this time—did you know?"

I shook my head.

"I don't feel like you're my real dad."

"I'm not. Mickey Fahey was." I handed him a picture I carried in my wallet—Rhiann, Jimmy, and Mickey. Happy. I added, "But I've always loved your mother."

"Then why'd you leave her?"

"I had to go. She couldn't wait for me." I shrugged. It really wasn't important now.

"If my dad hadn't died would you have..." He seemed unsure how to put it.

"Surfaced?"

"Yeah."

"Probably not."

"What would you have done?"

"Probably gone on as I did when he was alive. Kept my distance." Enjoyed the Fahey family's happiness vicariously.

"But if you always loved my mother, how could you stand to not be with her?"

How indeed?

"You didn't ask to be born. And you didn't get to pick your parents. But you deserved to have a decent life, two parents who could care for you, a stable environment. I couldn't give you those. Billy would have, if he'd lived. And Mickey did. All I could have done would be confuse things."

I was confusing him now, but he'd get over it.

"I don't see how you could have knocked her up and just left."

"Don't you? If you hadn't survived crashing your car, where do you think Beth would be?"

"You weren't in any crash!"

"Before I met your mother my life was one big crash. If I hadn't left when I did, I'd have ended up in prison for murder. Where would she have been then?"

He thought about that for a while. "Are you telling me this is like Oedipus?"

"The truth usually sets you free, but sometimes it can fuck with your mind."

"I think it's gonna take me a while to get used to all this."

"You've got the rest of your life."

"What are you gonna be doin'?"

"I'm going to ask your mother to marry me."

"What if I'm not okay with that?"

I shrugged. "I'm not telling *you* who you can marry."

He nodded as if that seemed fair. "Jesus! Now I got a family to support! Do I still have a job?"

"As long as it doesn't interfere with your grades."

"What if it does?"

"You may have to ask your new stepdad to help you out."

"You sound like you're pretty sure she'll marry you."

"I guess I'm pretty sure she will."

Rhiann

Our street is called Cemetery Road because it meanders in wide switchbacks between two cemeteries situated on broad natural terraces. Below them, the slope drops steeply to the river, and the road zigzags down to Overlook. The Catholics are laid out in the lower curve of one of the meanders, next to their church. Union Cemetery is across the road and straight downhill from us.

Mickey's buried there.

He and I used to sit on our porch, evenings, sharing our days and a cold beer—or hot chocolate, depending on the season—enjoying the peace. He'd told me on more than one occasion that he'd like to spend eternity here. And so he will, in a plot just below our porch. I was able to see it now that the trees had lost their leaves.

I'd been walking down to visit him, periodically, since he died, to catch him up on how we're doing. Mickey was a generous man, an old soul. He'd have been happy to hear that Smoke returned, that he and I had found each other. So after I accepted John's proposal, I headed down to share the news with Mickey.

And to say good-bye. I could let him go now; I had some kind of closure. All the persons missing from my life were accounted for. I was ready to start fresh.

It was nearly dark. Jimmy and Beth had gone off to a school dance. John was making a few business calls. I put on a sweater, put my flashlight in my pocket, and took the shortcut. Carrying a pot of red chrysanthemums, I squeezed through a gap in the cemetery fence.

I put the flowers down. I sat next to the headstone and told Mickey about my summer. About Beth and Jimmy. About John. I said good-bye.

When I got up to go, I noticed someone silhouetted against the last of the light. As he came near, he reached up and tipped his baseball cap.

He had just passed me, and I was stepping onto the shortcut path, when he whirled around and grabbed me.

"You ruined my life, bitch. You're gonna pay."

Rory Sinter!

"Then I'm gonna finish what I started with your brat."

John

I saw Rhiann leave her house and cross the street to visit Mickey. I wasn't spying this time; I didn't mean to intrude. But something made me follow. I took the same shortcut through the cemetery fence and picked my way down between the trees buttressing the slope. I stopped where the path flattened out on the nearly level graveyard.

In the waning light, I could see two figures among the markers. Rhiann knelt by Mickey's grave, her back to the road. The second figure was a man moving purposefully in her direction, silent as a ghost.

I'd seen that shade before, casting a pall over our summer—Rory Sinter.

Sudden panic made me plunge toward them. Quietly—to warn Rhiann was to forearm him.

Sinter tipped his cap as he approached her. Her body language broadcast inattention. She nodded and turned to come back home. He pounced on her from behind.

I ran.

He started dragging her toward the road. Rhiann struggled briefly, but he had her by the throat. She sagged in his grip. He let her drop.

As I closed the distance between us, my footfalls seemed to boom across the grass.

Sinter looked up and froze. The last glimmer of light reflected from the metal in his hand. A gun.

Fear for Rhiann made me light-headed. Rage spurred me on.

Sinter said, "Stop!"

Instead, I lunged at him.

The gun discharged. My shoulder struck his beltline. He fell back, with most of me on top. A metallic clatter signaled that he'd dropped the weapon.

We wrestled and flailed at one another, two dark figures against a darker ground. Headstones and markers surrounded us like ghostly witnesses.

Sinter rolled under me. I lost my balance. He shoved and

kicked, and scrambled out of reach, out of sight in the dark.

I heard his labored breathing and moved toward the sound. I heard him move away, saw his silhouette against the pale background of a headstone. There was a brushing sound as he felt in the grass for his pistol.

Then a light—like an airport beacon in the darkness—pinned him to a gravestone. He had the gun again. A semiautomatic. He aimed at me.

The light went off just before the gun did. Muzzle flare marked his location. I charged again and knocked him sideways. But I tripped and lost my balance.

He must have located me by sound. The cold finger of the muzzle poked my chest. Sinter said, "Move a hair and you're dead."

I lay still as a corpse.

He yelled, "You with the flashlight. Turn it on yourself and come over here or I'll shoot this asshole."

There was no light. No reply.

Sinter straddled me and leaned his weight on the gun, digging the muzzle into my sternum.

Pain cut through the red haze. Carl's words damped my rage—something he'd told me about semiautos. "You can't fire them with the slide pushed back."

As Sinter peered nervously into the darkness, I grabbed his pistol with both hands—pulled with one, pushed with the other—and rolled. He lost his balance and fell away.

And I had the gun.

I couldn't see him but I said, "Don't move, Sinter, or I'll shoot you."

And there was light. It pinned Sinter against a monument.

I said, "Who's there?"

Rhiann said, "It's me, John."

Something like despair crossed Sinter's face. He looked old and evil in the harsh glare. He stared into the light, then at me in the reflection from the marker. He said, "You're not gonna shoot me." He started backing away.

I was tempted, but I lowered the gun.

He kept looking back as he bolted. Rhiann kept him in the flashlight beam. So we saw clearly—when he ran toward Mickey's grave—what *he* didn't see: the pot of red flowers.

He tripped on it and fell forward. His skull glanced off the headstone. He landed on the grave, head at a peculiar angle against the marker. His wide eyes didn't blink. He didn't move. He didn't breathe.

Behind me, Rhiann said, "Oh, God!"

I turned and took the flashlight from her shaking hand. I realized I was still holding the gun. I put it on the grass and gave Rhiann a little hug.

"Stay here."

"Where—"

Keeping the light on Sinter, I stepped around to feel his neck for a pulse. A formality. It was obvious from the angle of his head that his neck was broken.

Rhiann said, "Is he…?"

"Dead."

In the light reflecting from Mickey's headstone she seemed more shocked than relieved.

I walked back to her and took her arm. "Let's go."

"Where?"

"Come on."

"We can't leave him there. On—" She couldn't bring herself to finish.

But I understood. "Mickey won't mind. It's just until the police finish."

"Oh, God." Rhiann was the toughest woman I've ever known, but she started sobbing.

I held her for a little while, then said, "C'mon, Rhi."

She sniffled and nodded, then let me lead her up the hill.

Rhiann

We waited for the police at my house. Sheriff Linden picked us up himself and drove us to the cemetery—I couldn't think of it as a *crime scene*. He wouldn't let us talk about what happened until we got there and he had us locked in separate squad cars. If John was worried, it didn't show.

I watched the cops go over the grave site with cameras and tape measures, and make diagrams before they took Rory away. Then they walked John—literally—through his version of events. I watched from the other squad car as the sheriff and state police investigator questioned John. And then they did the same with me. Checking to see if our stories matched.

It would've been terrifying if I weren't Mickey's widow. Long ago, he'd explained how police investigations work.

The investigator's name was Crowley, and he'd been called in because the deceased had been a deputy sheriff. There was more to it than that, but I knew they wouldn't tell us.

When they were satisfied with our version of the tragedy, Crowley drove us home. "You'll have to come in tomorrow and sign statements. For now you're in the clear. It looks as if Sinter's bad acts just caught up with him."

John agreed. "Bad karma."

Jimmy

Thanksgiving Day was in the sixties, so Beth and I sat on the porch with John and Steve.

I'd gotten Ma's old yearbooks out of the attic so I could show Beth pictures of her dad, Billy, Steve, and John when they were young.

She paged through the book until she came to the inside back cover, to a drawing of a fat, bowlegged frog with a cigarette dangling from its mouth. The inscription read, "Have a hoppy summer, Rhi. ILU. Smoke."

"Smoke?"

"What they used to call John in high school," Steve told her.

"Really? Why?"

John just shrugged, so Steve told her. She thought it was pretty funny. John looked embarrassed, which Steve seemed to think was a gas.

Just then, Ma came out to tell us dinner was ready.

We all filed into the dining room where Ma had set the table with her good china. She's a great cook, and the turkey looked like straight out of a cooking show.

After we said grace, Ma said, "John and I are getting married." She held up her left hand to show us a gold ring with a little jade frog instead of a diamond.

"Congratulations." Steve gave her a sad smile and held

his water glass up in a toast. "About time."

"What's with frogs?" Beth asked.

"You know the fairy tale about the frog prince?" John said.

Beth nodded.

"Years ago Jimmy's mother kissed me, and I turned into a human being. We're finally going to live happily ever after."

More from Michael Allen Dymmoch

The Fall

How far would you go to save your life and your world?

After a nasty divorce, single mother Joanne Lessing finally has her life together, and she's made a name for herself as a photographer. Then, while on assignment, she witnesses a hit and run. Property damage only. No big deal, she thinks. So she does the right thing—calls the cops. Joanne is dismayed when FBI agents arrive with the local detective. They admit the hit and run driver was a mob killer fleeing the scene of his latest hit. Joanne is relieved to find she can't really identify the hit man.

But when she sees the killer again while on another assignment, she takes his picture and finds her new life and her son's future threatened. Caught between the Mob and the FBI, she's on her own...

Death in West Wheeling

When a local schoolteacher disappears from rural West Wheeling, acting sheriff Homer Deters investigates. Before long he's got three more missing persons, two unidentified bodies, a car theft, a twenty-three-vehicle pile-up in the center of town, a missing tiger, and a squad of agitated ATF agents to deal with.

With no help from the Feds, Homer turns to his buddy, Rye Willis, and West Wheeling's eccentric postmistress, Nina Ross, to locate the missing, identify the bodies, and bring a murderer to justice. Packed with regional charm and Deters' wit, *Death in West Wheeling* shows how wild one case can get.

The Cymry Ring

Ian Carreg is a charming, canny detective with a career he loves and grown children he adores. He's come to terms with the death of his beloved wife and he's looking forward to the birth of his first grandchild. Jemma Henderson, on the other hand, is the beautiful daughter of a famous physicist, a skilled surgeon, and a convicted killer.

When Ian pursues Jemma to Cymry Henge, an ancient stone monument, he is sucked into her escape, and awakes in Roman Britain in the year 60 A.D. Ian and Jemma come face to face with both Celts and Romans, and Ian begins to doubt his own sanity—all he wants is to return home. But as they work together, Ian comes to accept the truth and convinces Jemma to help him foil a plot that could radically alter history.

Caleb & Thinnes Mysteries

The Man Who Understood Cats

Two unlikely partners join forces to solve a murder disguised as suicide and catch a killer ready to strike again.

Gold Coast psychiatrist Jack Caleb is wealthy, cultured, and gay. When one of his clients is found dead in a locked apartment—apparently from a self-inflicted wound—burned-out Chicago detective John Thinnes doesn't believe it was suicide. And Caleb is inclined to agree.

But Thinnes regards a shrink who makes house calls suspicious and starts his murder investigation with the doctor himself. An attack on Caleb that's made to look like an accidental drug overdose starts to change the detective's mind.

Soon, the two men find themselves a whirlwind of theft, scandal, and blackmail. Forced into an unlikely partnership, they'll have to confront not only a killer, but hard truths within themselves that will change them forever.

The Death of Blue Mountain Cat

The art world is the backdrop when a controversial artist reaches the end of his fifteen minutes of fame.

Native American artist Blue Mountain Cat has a style described as "Andy Warhol meets Jonathan Swift in Indian country." When he's murdered at an exclusive showing in a conservative art museum, Detective John Thinnes has no shortage of suspects. Targets of the artist's satire included a greedy developer, a beautiful Navajo woman, and black-market antiquities dealers. Even the victim's wife merits investigation.

Thinnes drafts psychiatrist Jack Caleb to guide him through the terra incognita of the art world, and their investigation turns up a desperate museum director, a savage critic, a married mistress, and shady dealings by the artist's partner. Thinnes and Caleb connect several apparently unrelated deaths as they follow leads from Wisconsin to Chicago's South Side and the mystery's explosive conclusion.

Incendiary Designs

Arson, passion, and religious fanaticism set Chicago ablaze in the deadliest summer on record.

While jogging through Chicago's Lincoln Park, Dr. Jack Caleb runs into murder—a mob setting a police car on fire—with the officer still inside. Caleb rescues the man, but later the cop's partner is found stoned to death. Detective John Thinnes is assigned to investigate.

Evidence points toward members of a charismatic church, but too many of them die in arson fires before the cops can round them up. When arson kills the apparent ring leader, it's too much coincidence. The remaining cop killers plead guilty; the case seems to be closed. But as Chicago heats up in the deadliest summer on record, it becomes clear that a serial arsonist is still at large.

A physician friend of Caleb's is implicated when some of the fire victims are found to have been drugged. To exonerate the man, Caleb sets a trap for the killer, and Thinnes and Caleb are nearly incinerated when the doctor's trap brings the case to a fiery finish.

The Feline Friendship

When a vicious rapist crosses the line into murder, Detective John Thinnes and his prickly new partner draft psychiatrist Jack Caleb to help them track the killer down.

When a young woman is brutally raped in the posh Lincoln Park neighborhood, Chicago Police detective John Thinnes catches the case—even though Thinnes hates working rapes. Worse yet, he has to deal with a new female detective who has a chip on her shoulder the size of a 12 gauge shotgun.

A second victim is murdered, and the rapes become "heater cases." What started as a simple investigation, soon twists around earlier, similar crimes. Tempers flare; the detective squad polarizes across the gender line. Dr. Jack Caleb, a psychiatrist and police consultant, is asked to mediate. But Thinnes's sometime-ally finds himself with conflicts of interest occasioned by their friendship and Caleb's own disturbing case load.

The investigation ranges from Chicago's Lincoln Park to the northern Illinois city of Waukegan. And the explosive climax explores not only the karma of evil but the beginning of a beautiful Feline Friendship.

White Tiger

The murder of a Vietnamese woman in Chicago's Uptown neighborhood brings Caleb and Thinnes together to catch a deadly criminal known only as the White Tiger.

The TV news report of a woman's murder in Uptown flashes psychiatrist Dr. Jack Caleb back to his time in Vietnam.

Assigned to investigate, Chicago detectives John Thinnes and Don Franchi find the victim's son curiously unmoved by his mother's death. Their preliminary canvass of the dead woman's neighborhood reveals that she was well liked and well off, and she had never quarreled with anyone but her "good son."

When Thinnes realizes that he knew the victim when he was stationed in Vietnam—twenty-four years earlier—he is pulled off the case. But Thinnes can't let go. And when a schizophrenic man shows up at Mrs. Lee's wake, connecting the deceased to another Vietnam vet and to an unsolved murder in wartime Saigon, Thinnes starts a retrospective investigation of that crime, soliciting Caleb's help to discover the identity of the White Tiger and set a trap for the elusive killer.

Printed in the USA
CPSIA information can be obtained
at www.ICGtesting.com
JSHW031710140824
68134JS00038B/3623